THE CASE OF THE DROP-DEAD DAME

RUBY MARTIN MYSTERY #1

BETH BRINKMEYER

Cinnamon Cozies

BONUS: GET 3 FREE BOOKS!

Cuddle up with more fun and quirky cozies right now!
Get 3 totally FREE cozy novellas:

Visit cinnamoncozies.com/bonus to claim your freebies!

1. Catnip & Culprits: A Pets Reporter Mystery

A small-town pets journalist gets her first taste of amateur sleuthing — and a taste of just how pets-crazed her hometown has become.

2. Fangs & Fairy Dust: Priscilla Pratt Mystery #0

A vampire baker —before she opened shop — sinks her teeth into a local mystery.

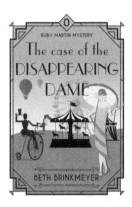

3. The Case of the Disappearing Dame: A Ruby Martin Mystery

A 1920s historical cozy in which the heroine must prove her mystery-solving skills when a young girl disappears at the fair.

Download all 3 books for free

at

www.cinnamoncozies.com/bonus

Thanks for reading :)

CONTENTS

CHAPTER ONE

Port Vernon, Michigan - November 1924

I chewed the inside of my bottom lip, my thumb running almost subconsciously over the darned hole in my left glove. The train's brakes squealed as it began its arrival in Port Vernon. It was such an important day in my life and yet, somehow, the weather hadn't decided to celebrate. My eyes skimmed the dirty piles of snow left over from an early storm, railway workers wearing worn overalls, and rundown buildings whose paint had long since given up and flaked away. As far as grand welcomings went, this was not one for the books.

Still, my heart leapt when the train finally lurched to a stop and the conductor announced, "Port Vernon!" This was it—a new chapter of my life was beginning. It didn't matter that I was only here because my father's new church had a one-bedroom parsonage for him and Mother with no room for me. As it was, my younger brother would have to sleep in the living room when he was on breaks from school. It didn't matter that I was 20 years old or that my hand-me-down traveling suit had last been at the height of fashion when McKinley was president.

I had to give myself a firm talking to as I stepped down from the train, hatbox and purse in one hand, carpetbag in the other. In fact, I was so busy trying to convince myself that my out-of-fashion outfit didn't matter in the least that I turned abruptly and ran smack into someone.

"Oof," I grunted, and tried to get my footing without dropping my bags.

A strong arm caught mine and I looked up into warm, chocolatey brown eyes that twinkled at me. A dark curl hung down under his newsboy cap. His nose was a little too big, but it only served to add character to his face. His complexion was dark enough to reveal Southern- or Eastern-European ancestry.

"Are you okay?" he asked, the corner of his mouth curling a little.

I nodded, eyes wide. "S-sorry," I stuttered.

"No problem. I never mind bumping into a good-looking doll."

It was such an obvious line that I should have brushed him off and yet I couldn't stop my heart from fluttering and my lips from smiling back at him.

"What's your name, kid?" he asked, finally righting me and taking his hand from my arm.

"I'm Ruby Martin." I remembered my manners in a sudden, embarrassed moment and thrust out my hand to shake, flustered all over again.

He smirked and said, "Gus Jones. Good to meet you."

At exactly that moment, my Aunt Muriel's shrill voice pierced the air around us and Gus dropped my hand, looking around in surprise.

"Ruby Martin, whatever are you doing with that

scoundrel?" She burst from the crowd, the large bird of prey perched upon her hat glaring down at us.

I took a deep breath, steeled myself, and tried not to look guilty. "Hello, Aunt Muriel." My nervous smile flickered in her direction and died under her fierce glare.

I'd been prepared for a different life than the cheerful one I'd had with my parents and younger brother, Robert. Living with a maiden aunt was sure to be quieter, with new routines to learn and rules to follow. Unfortunately, my Aunt Muriel, my mother's older sister, was immediately proving to be something else entirely. She had never married and was, I was sorry to see, the very picture of a spinster aunt, tall and spare. Her hair was a shade of blonde that made the gray feel right at home. Though her dark eyes snapped and her complexion was good, everything about my aunt made her seem elderly including her sensible lace-up boots, which ended primly at the hem of her long skirts, and the warning glances she shot at any young man who drifted too close in the crowd.

Not for the first time, I wished that we'd met more than the three times I could remember. Maybe I would have been more resistant to leaving my family's nest. Maybe it would have been worth sharing the sofa bed with Robert after all.

I took a deep breath, steeled myself, and tried not to look guilty. "Hello, Aunt Muriel." My nervous smile flickered in her direction and died under her fierce glare.

"I bumped into Gus, here, and he was kind enough to help me get steady on my feet." I made a point not to look at him so that I wouldn't blush again.

"Well, thank you for your help, young man," Aunt

Muriel peered at him over low glasses, doing her best imitation of a disapproving schoolmarm. "You can be on your way now. Let's get your trunk, Ruby."

"Welcome to town, kid," Gus said with a wink before turning and sauntering off.

I suppressed a sigh as Aunt Muriel turned on her heel and stomped off, her shoulders hunched and her pocketbook gripped under one arm with all the force of a vise. Purse thieves didn't stand a chance against her.

"You there," she barked at a porter who had the misfortune of lounging against a counter. "Get this girl's trunk."

Fumbling in my purse, I pulled out my ticket stub and tried to offer the man an apologetic smile. He merely shot Aunt Muriel an angry parting glance and tromped off to retrieve my trunk from the train platform.

Once the porter returned, wheeling a squeaking cart which carried my battered steamer trunk, Aunt Muriel led the way to where a very skinny horse and wagon stood. I glanced around as the porter waited for a tip and Aunt Muriel determinedly ignored him. There were no other horses and wagons here. Several different automobiles were sitting in the cold, waiting for their owners to return. I climbed up onto the seat with just the faintest tingle of embarrassment around the edges of my ears.

I'd never been too proud to ride in such an outdated form of transportation when Dad had a church in the Illinois countryside. Still, it would have been so much more fitting to arrive at my new life in a shiny red sedan, a luxurious cashmere car blanket tucked across my lap. Of course, to make that dream fit, I would need a fur coat and shoes that weren't ugly, functional, and almost worn through at the toes.

Aunt Muriel climbed into the seat with a grunt,

snapped the reins, and clucked to the nag. He glanced back at us as though to make sure we really meant it before breaking into a steady clop.

"This is the bad part of town." My aunt began to narrate our journey home without preamble. "The train station is close to the river and all the riffraff lives here. Canada is over that way." She pointed a gloved finger towards the ribbon of gray water that peeked through the buildings. "That's the Detroit River. Ferries go across it daily, though why anyone would want to go to Canada, I can't imagine."

I pursed my lips. If I was expected to have a reply, I didn't any idea where to begin. Luckily, my aunt didn't need any comments from me.

"That's Tucker Street. It leads to Main Street. Most people like to throw their money away at Decker Grocery as though it grows on trees." She snorted. "We do most of our marketing at Santoro's Grocery. They tried to cheat me once, but I told Mr. Santoro a thing or two and they've treated me fairly ever since. I can even get stale bread there for two cents a loaf."

What did she need stale bread for? Would I be expected to live on it? Or did my aunt have a secret love of feeding ducks? I'd known that my mother was gifted when it came to pinching pennies. Now I had a new understanding of where she'd learned it from.

The sound of a horn made me jump, though it had no impact whatsoever on my aunt or the tired horse. A moment later, a car chugged around us, the driver shaking his fist and shouting something I couldn't understand.

I drooped in humiliation, but Aunt Muriel was the picture of prim self-righteousness. Her back was ramrod straight; her eyes never left the horse's back. Once the car careened around a corner and out of sight, she sniffed in disdain and continued her diatribe as though she hadn't been interrupted.

"I hope you're not one of those flappers, Ruby. I can't abide that wasteful foolishness. Your mother assures me that you are a sensible girl who isn't given to flights of fancy. I expect you to be quiet, tidy, and frugal." Her mouth settled into the thinnest of lines for a moment. "You might as well know that my brother, Howard, pays my bills. It's only right that he should care for his older sister. Still, I don't take his sacrifice for granted and neither should you. It's likely you'll be a spinster, too, living off the charity of your family. It's time that you learn how to make the most of the hand you've been dealt."

I worked to keep my face calm while my insides clenched and a rock slid down my chest and sank into my stomach. I wanted to make a loud declaration that I was not going to be a spinster and possibly even make a run back to the train station.

Of course, making an enemy of my aunt was not wise. However, I did begin to tune out her continuing lecture on how to keep our expenses low.

The houses changed from small, spare, worn dwellings to more attractive and roomy places. Aunt Muriel turned the wagon onto Third Street and I was surprised to see that the homes in this part of town were large, with neat yards. Surely my aunt didn't live here. I couldn't reconcile these large houses with the woman who sat beside me explaining that she kept her house cold because too much heat was not good for the health or the pocketbook.

All confusion was resolved when the wagon took one more turn down a narrow alley and we passed a few garages and smaller homes tucked in the gaps. The wagon stopped before one such dwelling. Beyond it, a much larger brick house sat majestically, its backyard separating it from the little cottage. I followed my aunt's lead and climbed down from the wagon, taking in my new home. It was a two-story A-frame structure with wood shingles on the bottom and a Tudor-style trimming along the attic. Considering that the sky was gray and the only leaves clinging to the trees were brown and shriveled, I thought that the house was decidedly friendly.

"Can you manage your trunk?" Aunt Muriel called.

I nodded and went to lift it down from the back of the wagon.

"Go on in. I have to fetch Nelson to care for the horse." And she stomped off, shoulders hunched, down the alley.

I sighed and walked up the packed-earth track that led to the front door. It was nice to have a moment alone to take in my new home. Once my trunk, hatbox, and carpetbag were all stacked neatly in the front hall, I took off my hat and gloves and looked around.

Inside the front door, the living room was immediately to the right, a hall led straight back to the kitchen, and a staircase headed upstairs along the left wall of the hallway. I walked through the living room, taking in the few furniture pieces that failed to fill the room as well as the complete lack of even a speck of dust. Behind this room was a dining area which made up for the sparse furnishings in the previous room with an overwhelming amount of potted ferns. I continued forward, through to a butler's pantry and into the kitchen. The theme of minimalistic design and almost religious cleanliness had been carried out throughout the entire floor. I was considering going back to examine the sun room hidden behind two French doors off the living room when the kitchen door opened and Aunt Muriel arrived.

"Have you seen everything down here?" She waited for my nod. "Grab your things and I'll show you upstairs."

Our shoes thudded as we climbed the creaking staircase to the second floor. I was shown the linen closet, bathroom, and three bedrooms, one of which was filled with all the knitting paraphernalia that Aunt Muriel required for her lone hobby.

"My women's group knits scarves, mittens, hats, and blankets for the poor. During the war, we made a great number of bandages to send overseas," she explained before opening the last door. I got the impression that having such a large stash of yarn would otherwise be too wasteful, but the fact that it was for charity justified the excess. "This will be your room. I use the one closest to the bathroom because I'm up throughout the night at my age." Aunt Muriel looked around the room with satisfaction. "I'll leave you to unpack. Supper will be in an hour."

A brass bedstead, battered end table, and enormous wooden bureau were all the furniture this room apparently required. The room itself was large and the furniture seemed oddly sad, like three girls at a dance who were hoping to be noticed but were surprised to spend the whole night as wallflowers.

Unpacking was fast; I only had a few dresses to hang in the closet. My underclothes didn't come close to filling the deep bureau drawers, even when I added my sweaters, blouses, and skirts. The room did feel better, though, once I put my brush and comb set out, placed my books on the table next to the bed, and stood a framed photograph of my family in a place of honor.

I would have felt funny if I stayed in my room much

longer once I'd finished unpacking, so I made my way back downstairs and offered to help Aunt Muriel with supper. During our preparations for the meal, I was treated to another lecture on how to make our meager rations stretch. I also learned that the stale bread was not for feeding the birds, as I'd begun to hope. It turned out Aunt Muriel found it a beneficial ingredient in a number of casseroles.

Supper was filling, if a bit bland. I supposed that spices were a frivolous luxury we spinsters couldn't afford. To my relief, the staleness of the bread in the chicken casserole was barely noticeable and I made a mental note to remember the trick should I ever become as financially strained as Aunt Muriel.

I was allowed to wash the dishes, though I received a chastising when I used too much soap and again when I went to toss the water into the yard. Apparently even the dirty dishwater could have another life and I left it for the next day, slightly worried as to how it might be used again.

To my disappointment, I learned that Aunt Muriel didn't have a radio. Though not keen on many modern trends, I was terribly fond of the wireless. Even Dad enjoyed sitting down in the evening and listening to his favorite programs, and he was as old-fashioned as they came.

Bedtime came early for my aunt. After an hour of knitting and further lectures, this time on the trouble with current fashions and "girls today," the clock struck eight and she briskly returned her project to its basket by her chair and got to her feet.

"Don't stay up too late. Tomorrow's washing day and I'll need your help. Breakfast is at seven." And she was gone.

I chuckled to myself as I listened to her feet moving about upstairs. I hadn't said more than a dozen words since

I'd arrived. It was funny in that moment, but later, when I was shivering in bed, I worried that I was beginning a new, dark chapter of my life. Was I to spend the next years trailing after Aunt Muriel, following her to her women's group and being subjected to her endless lecturing? What a dreadful thought.

And I suppose things might have turned out just that way if not for the events of the next day. I'd finished a breakfast of one fried egg over stale toast with the barest scraping of marmalade, then moved on to helping wash Aunt Muriel's laundry. The previous night's dishwater had been reheated and used again to wash the breakfast dishes before I was allowed to throw it out. This was a great relief to me since I'd grown a bit nervous that it would be used to wash the laundry. I could only imagine climbing into bed and finding dried food bits stuck to the sheets.

As you can guess, the washing consisted of a scant amount of strong lye soap, hot water that was probably left over from the previous week's washing, and a few items of actual wash. Aunt Muriel's woolen stockings, long, flannel union suit, and thick, itchy underclothes joined one set of bedsheets, one worn bath towel, and the kitchen towels. I received a thorough explanation of exactly how I was to wash each item, send it through the wringer, and then hang it outside on the line to dry.

It was a relief, again, to find myself alone. Hanging clothes was a duty that couldn't be muffed too badly, and so I was allowed to do it unsupervised on my very first day in town. After struggling to pin up the damp items in the biting end-of-November wind, I began to suspect that I'd been given this task due to its sheer unpleasantness.

As I wrestled the wet bedsheet onto the front line so as to hide Aunt Muriel's unmentionables from the eyes of passing neighbors, a car pulled to a stop behind me.

"Hello," a female voice called.

I turned and saw a dark-eyed, dark-haired young woman, wearing a fashionable cloche and thick fur coat, sitting in the passenger side of a shiny new automobile. Next to her, a handsome blond young man grinned at me.

"Hello," I said, feeling a little shy. I wrapped my arms around myself to ward off the chill and walked closer to the car.

"Do you live with Miss Barnes? Or are you just working for her?" the young woman asked, her head cocked to the side as though she was some sort of little bird.

"She's my aunt. My name is Ruby Martin and I've come to live with her for a time."

The young woman sat up and bounced in her seat. "Oh, how too, too divine! I'm Dora Beaumont, and this is my brother Charlie. We live in that big house right there. Miss Barnes rents this cottage from our father."

I nodded with understanding and allowed their house a quick look. It was the big brick one that dwarfed Aunt Muriel's house. No wonder Dora could afford such a glorious fur coat. My eyes went back to the pair in the automobile and I found that Charlie was looking at me intently. I'm sure I blushed, though, thankfully, the cold wind had already reddened my cheeks. I wasn't accustomed to admiring looks from fashionable men.

"You must come to visit me just as soon as you can," Dora went on. "I'm sure we'll be very good friends. And to think that I met you first. The gang will be positively green with envy that I have the scoop on the new gal in town. Well, Charlie and I have to split. Mother wants us at an awful charity event today. Can you come by tomorrow? Just walk through that gate there and right up to the back door. I sleep in until at least ten, though, so don't come over too early."

The car roared away and I was left waving at Dora, who leaned out the window, grinned, and waved back.

"With neighbors like you," I said to no one, "there's no way that living in Port Vernon will be dull."

There was no way to know just how right I was on that point.

CHAPTER TWO

Nervously, I lifted the latch and entered the Beaumont's backyard the next morning. Even though Dora had invited me, I still felt like I was intruding. My heart pounded as I imagined her staring at me in embarrassment as I walked into her home, never having actually meant for me to take her invitation so literally. I braced myself for such an eventuality and told myself sternly that it wouldn't matter. Surely Port Vernon was large enough that I could avoid Dora if I humiliated myself in front of her on my second day in town.

To my great relief, she acted just as excited to see me today as she had been the previous day. I sank onto the settee next to her and tried not to grin foolishly as Dora began to tell me about her plans for that evening.

"It's going to be a simply divine get-together," she cooed. "You'll have to come along. You do have better glad rags than that old thing, don't you?"

I looked down at my out-of-fashion brown dress and shook my head. Dora fell into raptures about how sad it was.

To be honest, I think I was shaking my head about going to a party with her. Meeting lots of new people made me nervous, but the possibility of shyness didn't seem to occur to my new friend.

"Never mind. I have a light blue silk that will make you the envy of all the gals. You'll see." She patted my hand as though the matter was settled. "I wore it to Mother's dull charity event back in September, but none of the kids were there, so they won't be any the wiser."

It pained me to do it, but I had to speak up. "I don't think I can go to a party tonight. My aunt would never allow it."

Dora's dark eyes grew wide and filled with sorrow. "Golly, Ruby, you're practically a nun."

"Hardly." I waved that off with a chuckle. "But I don't want to upset Aunt Muriel right after I've arrived." I almost sagged with relief that I'd thought up a good excuse. The last thing I wanted was for Dora to think I was a wet blanket, but I really and truly didn't want to go to the party.

"Tell her you're spending the evening visiting friends with me. It's the truth, isn't it? Old spinsters like your aunt like it when their young relatives are accepted into my crowd. I don't mean to boast, but around here, I'm the berries." She preened a little and I admit that I was a tad envious of her at that moment. What would it be like to have a closet full of beautiful dresses and dozens of friends?

Dora tossed her hair and added, "Popularity means everyone wants you to like them, even old ladies."

She was completely confident that this plan would work and no amount of subtle hedging on my part dissuaded her. In fact, she insisted on walking over to the house and convincing Aunt Muriel to let me spend the evening with her. I was a little disappointed my aunt didn't put up more of a fight.

"And we'll have Ruby back at a decent hour," Dora concluded with a smile. "It's the perfect way to welcome her to Port Vernon."

"I suppose that would be nice," Aunt Muriel said, her lips thin. "A quiet get-together, you say? Who will be chaperoning?"

"It's a friend from our church and I believe both her parents will be there," Dora lied glibly.

Aunt Muriel nodded, though her sharp eyes raked Dora for any evidence of dishonesty. I guess Dora's bright smile and wide eyes betrayed nothing and my aunt gave her permission, much to my dismay.

Then we had to troop back across the yard to the Beaumont's so that Dora could force me to try on her dress of choice for me and then choose matching accessories. Considering that we couldn't be more different, Dora's dress looked good on me. She was petite and curvy, with dark hair and eyes. Where she was pale, I was more tanned. Though I was taller and slimmer, her dress still fit me fairly well. It set off my blonde hair and brown eyes nicely. In many ways, Dora and I were opposites. Still, we spent a very pleasant afternoon with Dora dressing my hair amid many sighs and not-so-subtle comments about how it would be more fashionable if I bobbed it.

By the time supper came and went, I was jittery. I'd never been to a party before and was envisioning any number of humiliations. After we pulled on our coats Dora sized up my mended hand-me-down wool coat and insisted I change into one of her furs. Then we were on our way.

Dora spent the walk to the party filling me in on all the

hijinks she'd gotten into with the friends we were about to meet. She was so busy talking that she didn't notice my silence until we were several blocks from her house. "What's the matter, Ruby? You've been so quiet."

I tried not to sound as bent out of shape as I felt. "I don't think I'm going to the party tonight after all. I should just go home." I tried not to sound as bent out of shape as I felt.

"You have to go! I want to introduce you to the whole gang," Dora pouted.

"I don't know," I mumbled, fiddling with my glove.

Dora's pout melted to a sudden smile. "Did I tell you that my brother will be there? He can keep an eye on things. You must come, Ruby, you must."

I'd always imagined going to a party like this, though I was much braver in my pretend world than I was in real life. And having a friend like Dora Beaumont was a dream come true. I was just so terribly aware of my shortcomings. Something in me was positive that I'd arrive at the party and everyone there would plainly see them. I told myself sternly that it was silly and then smiled nervously at Dora.

"All right. Let's go quickly, before I change my mind."

She squealed and hopped on the spot. "We'll have the most fun, Ruby!"

Which was how I found myself in a makeshift speakeasy my second night in Port Vernon. I could only imagine what my father would have said if he'd known what his daughter got up to just as soon as she was out of his sight.

Charlie pulled up in his car right as we turned down the street. We paused to wait for him to park and get out of the car, shivering all the while. He put out his elbows and both Dora and I slipped our hands through and let him lead us down to the house and through the door.

By the time we arrived, the band was playing a hot jazz number, people were dancing and laughing, and gin was being served generously from the kitchen.

"I'm off to get some giggle water," Dora called over the music. "Do you want some?"

Charlie assented as I shook my head. It was bad enough that I was in the same room as illegal alcohol. There was no way that I was going to drink any. I'd often heard my father preach against the evils of drunkenness and the importance of obeying our government's decision for Prohibition. Of course, I'd never actually had the opportunity to imbibe before, nor had I ever seen someone who was drunk.

I had a feeling that tonight I'd get plenty of chances to do both, though I planned to refuse the former every chance I got. The raucous crowd around me teemed with young people who were talking animatedly, and tossing back liberal amounts of clear liquid that was most definitely not water.

Dora turned to go and bumped into a red-haired flapper in a silver dress. The other girl registered who had knocked into her and her face grew hard. Similarly, Dora folded her arms across her full chest and her eyes narrowed.

"Jean Waldeck," she spat. "I guess they're letting just anyone into this party. It was smart of you to wear those paste pearls to a dive like this." She fingered own real pearls as she said it and flashed the girl a venomous smile.

Jean scowled, then cocked her head. "Nice dress, Dora. Too bad it looked better on the hanger."

Dora's face reddened, but she merely said, "Is your brother here, Jean?" Dora's eyes grew wide in mock embarrassment. "Oh, I forgot. He's in the nut house, isn't he?"

Jean's face turned scarlet and her eyes bugged as Dora smiled triumphantly. Then a secretive smile spread across

Jean's lips. "Is your pop here tonight? He's such a darling daddy; always so very sweet to me."

"Why, you ..." Dora leaned forward furiously, as though ready to attack.

The redhead smirked and brushed past her before sailing off into the other room. Once Jean was gone, Dora stomped into the kitchen. I turned to Charlie and asked, "What was that about?"

"Dora and Jean have hated each other since they were in grade school," he brushed it off. "Looks like there's a place to sit over there." And with that, he threaded his way through the crowd to an empty settee.

I didn't know what else to do, so I followed him and took the proffered seat. This noisy, gyrating crowd of young people was not who I'd previously imagined would toss away the law so easily. Always, my mind had conjured seedy men and shifty-eyed women who were passed out and depressed from their terrible choices. Everyone at this party was fashionable and seemingly having the time of their life. I watched them, feeling very young and naïve.

Soon, Dora returned with two glasses in her hands. Charlie took a healthy swig of his immediately. He had seemed straight-laced to me before this, but I began to wonder if my first impression of him had been wrong.

"Well, if it isn't Ruby Martin," a pleasant tenor sang into my ear, taking me completely by surprise.

I turned in my seat and my eyes locked with those of Gus Jones, who was grinning at me.

"Gus, what are you doing here?" I asked breathlessly.

"A friend of mine invited me." He walked around the couch and stood in front of me, looking between me and Charlie.

"This is Charlie Beaumont and this is his sister, Dora." I hastily made the introductions. "They're my aunt's neighbors. Charlie, Dora, this is Gus Jones. He and I met at the train station yesterday."

Dora giggled falsely and held out a hand for Gus to shake. The move irritated me and I chastised myself for it. I had no right to be jealous of Dora's bubbly personality and adorable appearance. Besides, I had no claim on Gus, nor was I likely ever to. Still, the way Dora batted her eyes at Gus made me grit my teeth.

Gus and Charlie shook hands, some mysterious male evaluation passing between them. Charlie was taller, better dressed, and handsome in a regal sort of way. Gus was shorter, broader through the shoulders, and his good looks made a girl want to take him home and tame him. I didn't know what the pair of them saw in each other after their hasty appraisal, but nothing further happened and Charlie gulped down more of his drink.

Gus turned to me and said, "So, Ruby, want to dance?"

I'm sure my eyes were the size of saucers. I knew how to waltz and do the foxtrot, but the frenzied movements coming from the dancefloor were foreign to me. "No thanks," I stammered.

"She's new to all this," Dora said. "You can push me around the floor, though."

Gus agreed and Dora knocked back her drink before taking his arm. I watched them go, my stomach sinking a little.

Charlie leaned over and said, "Is this really your first time at a place like this?"

Glumly, I said, "It sure is."

To my surprise, Charlie didn't make an excuse and find

some flapper to dance with. Instead, he scooted a little closer so we didn't have to yell over the noise and asked me about my parents. We filled the next twenty minutes with very pleasant conversation that left me extremely grateful to him.

"You've never even tried gin?" he asked, incredulous.

I was relaxed enough by then to grin and shake my head. "I don't even know where you would buy it."

"Do you see that fellow over there?" Charlie pointed through the crowd. "The one in the baggy suit and hat?"

Studiously, I looked where he was pointing until I spotted the man. "The one with Jean Waldeck?"

"That's the one. His name is Louis Hardy and he's a bootlegger."

"Really?" I gasped and craned my neck to get a better look.

Charlie smiled and nodded. "No fooling. He probably goes over to Canada and buys it there. Then he smuggles it back here at night."

I could hardly believe that I was in the presence of a real bootlegger. There was something wickedly exciting about doing something that would shock my parents.

Dora returned and introduced me to several friends who then whirled off with her to dance. Charlie nodded at several of his acquaintances, though he never left my side. After a while, he noticed that I was ready to leave and went off to find Dora.

"Oh, you don't want to go," she cried, weaving slightly. "The fun's just starting!"

"I'm going to take Ruby home," Charlie insisted. "We don't want her getting in trouble with her aunt."

Dora plastered a wet kiss on my cheek and begged me to

come over the next day. I bade her goodnight and Charlie and I headed out.

We kept up a friendly conversation all the way home. When the car pulled up in front of Aunt Muriel's house, I turned to him. "Thanks for everything, Charlie. I didn't think this night would be much fun, but, thanks to you, I had a good time."

He cocked his head and gave me a searching glance. "You know, Ruby, I had a good time, too. I'm glad you've moved to town. Dora could use a good influence like you."

I climbed out and waved to him, thinking that I might have also been a good influence on him. After all, Charlie had had only had one drink at the party.

However, the next day, when I finally made my way through the gate and into their kitchen, both Dora and Charlie were drinking cups of coffee and wincing at every loud noise. Apparently, Charlie had dropped me off and returned to the party. It was a blow to the smug self-satisfaction I'd been entertaining.

Mrs. Beaumont clacked into the room, the morning paper in her hands. Before I could make up my mind whether or not to scold her two older children, she declared, "Did you hear the news? Jean Waldeck was found dead this morning!"

The silence that followed Mrs. Beaumont's announcement was absolute. Charlie froze with a forkful of eggs halfway to his mouth and Dora sat with her coffee cup in the air.

"Jean was found dead?" Dora finally squeaked. "What

does that mean? Did someone do her in or was there an accident?"

I'd been wondering the same thing, though I'd at least had the good grace not to say it out loud. Still, when Mrs. Beaumont handed the newspaper to her children, I leaned forward intently, gripping my gloves tightly as I waited eagerly for Charlie to read the article aloud.

"It says that she was out for a walk last night," he paraphrased as his eyes scanned the article. *"Jean Waldeck, of 7 Maple Drive, daughter of Mr. and Mrs. Dennis Waldeck, was found dead in the alley off of Main Street by a passerby early on the morning of November 25th. A police representative stated that Miss Waldeck had been strangled in a robbery gone wrong."*

"You went to school with the Waldeck girl, didn't you, Dora?" Mrs. Beaumont asked in a distracted way as she poured herself a cup of coffee. "Isn't she the one with the brother in the sanatorium?"

Dora nodded dumbly, her eyes as big as saucers.

"Well, I'm off to the ladies' aid meeting. Don't forget to invite Ruby to the Christmas party." Mrs. Beaumont sailed out of the room in a move that reminded me strikingly of her daughter.

"Good golly," Dora finally whispered. "I can't believe Jean's dead!"

I picked up the paper the moment Charlie put it down and read the article for myself. "This information is wrong, though," I mused out loud. "Jean wasn't just out for a walk; she was at the same party we were. And it doesn't make sense that she would be robbed, since you said that her pearls were paste." I stared up at nothing for a minute, my mind whirling. Finally, I gave the elder Beaumont children a bracing look and announced, "I think we need to go to the police and tell them what we know."

Charlie laughed dryly. "We can't do that, Ruby."

"Why not?" I took a small step back in surprise.

"Because, silly, we were at the party, too." Dora said it as though she was explaining something very simple to a stupid child. "We can't tell the police we saw her there without getting ourselves in trouble."

"I didn't drink any alcohol," I explained. "I could tell them."

"You explain it to her," Dora sighed. "My brain is still waterlogged."

Charlie stood up and took his plate to the sink. "The police won't believe that you were there and didn't imbibe. Besides, it'll lead them to the rest of us and we'll all get in trouble."

"But a girl was murdered," I spluttered. "Don't you want to see her attacker brought to justice?"

Charlie shrugged. "That's the police's job. Not ours. Let them get to work on that and we'll stay out of their way. Look, I've got to run an errand for Dad. He's thinking about selling our boat and wants me to talk to someone about getting it repainted."

"Daddy's selling our boat? How dreadful! I'd march downtown to tell him he'd better not, but my head is splitting. I'm going back to bed," groaned Dora. "See you later, Ruby."

I watched her slink off to her room. Charlie shrugged again and tossed me his roguish grin before heading off to his own pursuits. Hackles up, I turned and stalked out of the kitchen, needing some space to clear my head. Rather than heading back to Aunt Muriel's, I walked in the other direction at a brisk pace.

It wasn't until almost fifteen minutes later that my brain stopped lurching from curiosity about Jean's death to frustration at Charlie and Dora's lack of concern. Raising a hand to keep the sun from my eyes, I looked around to get my bearings. I was back near the train station, I knew, since I could hear the sound of squealing brakes and see the river in the distance. There wasn't anywhere that I particularly needed to go, so I turned on my heel and began to backtrack.

"Hey there! Ruby!" a voice from behind me called.

There weren't many people who knew my name in Port Vernon and, besides, I knew this voice already. My cheeks flushed automatically as I turned and watched Gus Jones jog out from a side street to catch up with me.

"Howsa girl?"

I wrapped my arms around myself. "Did you hear about Jean Waldeck's death?"

The smile slipped from his face and Gus nodded seriously. "I did. That's nasty stuff."

"The police think that she was just out for a stroll last night and was robbed." I studied him out of the corner of my eyes.

He shot me an appraising glance. "We know for a fact that isn't true."

My tense stomach relaxed a tiny bit. At least he seemed to understand that something was amiss.

"I also don't think she was robbed, since she was wearing a fake necklace." We walked in silence a few minutes. Finally, my frustration with the Beaumonts could no longer be stemmed. "Dora and Charlie are more worried about their father selling the family boat than they are about finding Jean's killer. I'm so mad I could scream."

"Well, the rich are very different than you and me, old

girl," Gus shrugged. "I suppose to them their boat is more important than the life of some person they hardly knew."

"I don't understand that. How can anyone value things over a human being?" But his understanding seemed to help drain my anger of its potency. We walked quietly for a minute.

Gus broke the silence by saying, "Oh, hey, where's your coat? You must be freezing." Without asking, he slipped out of his own coat and tossed it around my shoulders.

I was instantly warmer, both inside and out. "Thanks."

"No problem." Gus gave me that half smile that made me melt inside a little.

"Did you know Jean at all?" I asked, forcing my mind off the pleasant, musky smell of the jacket, and back onto the problem at hand.

"Sure," he shrugged. "I suppose I knew her a bit. She was often at parties I went to."

"Is there some reason that someone would want her dead?" I reached up and fiddled with the charm of my birthstone necklace. "Did she have any enemies?"

Gus let out a low whistle. "That's some heavy stuff, baby. Are you thinking that someone killed Jean on purpose?"

It was my turn to shrug. "I don't know. But if it wasn't a robbery gone wrong, what really happened? What reason was there for Jean to be killed?"

"I'm not up on my Agatha Christie," he quipped.

I bristled slightly, afraid that he was mocking me. "Well, I am. And people aren't just killed without a reason. Even if it was an accident, there had to be a cause. The paper said that she was strangled, so someone had to be very angry or very afraid of Jean in order to kill her that way."

Gus rubbed his chin. "You're one smart cookie, did you know that?"

His words soothed my rumpled feelings and I smiled shyly at him. "I've always liked puzzles and mysteries and things like that. My father and I would work them together. I even solved a mystery at the county fair last year."

"No kidding? You figure out which judge at the cattle tent was crooked?" He said it with a smirk.

"I found a girl who'd been kidnaped," I responded proudly. Gus's expression turned from teasing to impressed and I felt my chest swell.

He whistled. "I always knew you were a smart cookie." We walked in silence for a few steps before he asked, "You on good terms with your old man?"

"Of course," I answered in surprise. "Aren't you?"

His humorless laugh answered that question even before he said, "My pops was a hard drinker who worked long hours at the factory. When he wasn't at work or at the bar, he was at home yelling at me or my mother or my sister."

"I'm sorry," I said contritely.

"He's been dead since I was a kid. It's not a big deal."

I opened my mouth to say something, but Gus cut me off. "So, you really think Jean's death was murder?"

"It has to be. Whether it was planned or not, someone meant to kill her. Since thieves usually carry a knife or gun to threaten their victims with, it just can't be a robbery."

"That makes sense." Gus and I turned down the alley towards Aunt Muriel's. "I suppose I could ask around and see if anyone knows anything."

"Really? That would be wonderful, Gus." We stopped at the corner of the garage and I handed his coat back.

"Sure, cookie, it isn't a big thing." He gave me a full

smile and slid his arms into his coat. "I'll let you know what I find out."

"Wonderful," I repeated. "Oh, and thanks for the use of your coat."

"Thanks for keeping it warm for me," he winked, and trotted off.

CHAPTER THREE

It was with an enormous amount of weary relief that I escaped my aunt's clutches the following morning and made my way through the gate and into the Beaumont's well-manicured backyard. Surprisingly, Aunt Muriel seemed glad that I had found a friend, unaware that the "get-together" I'd attended had been a party complete with booze and jazz. I managed to sit through her lecture on Dora's rumored flapper ways and how I must not let myself be influenced by such foolishness. I suppose that the idea of my being a millstone around her neck was somehow worse than my becoming a flapper, though, so Aunt Muriel allowed me to miss out on floor mopping.

"You'd just be in the way," she said in her clipped tone as I scooted out the door, too anxious to be gone to bother putting both arms in my coat before braving the cold air outside.

I could see movement behind the lace-trimmed curtain on the Beaumont's kitchen window. Even though I'd visited before, I was still hesitant to barge in. I lifted a hand and knocked as loudly as I dared. Only a moment later, a young girl's face appeared on the other side of the door. I looked at her with surprise, not having seen her during my previous visits.

"Hello? Are you with the police?" The girl's forehead furrowed as she looked me up and down. She had Dora's dark hair and pixie-like face but Charlie's steady gray eyes. This girl had to be a sister or possibly a cousin.

"The police?" I asked, completely at sea. "No, I'm Ruby Martin. I live next door with Miss Barnes. I'm here to visit Dora Beaumont."

She stepped back and motioned for me to enter. "I didn't really think you were with the police. For one thing, you aren't wearing a uniform. And, for another thing, I don't know if Mother called for them yet."

I raised my eyebrows and tried to see around her for any sign of trouble. "Oh, dear. Is something wrong?"

The girl opened her mouth but a whirlwind of noise and movement interrupted us as Dora burst into the room.

"Ruby, thank goodness you're here. You'll never believe what's happened! My pearl ring has gone missing and, I hate to even think it, but I'm afraid that our maid, Bessie, took it. What is this town coming to? First Jean was killed and now there's a thief in our house!"

"Why do you think Bessie took it?" I asked as she grabbed my arm and dragged me into the front parlor where she laid herself out dramatically on the sofa.

"I hardly know where to begin," Dora cried, and threw an arm over her eyes.

The younger girl who'd opened the kitchen door slunk quietly into the room and we exchanged a glance.

"When did you last see the ring?" I prompted, hoping to be helpful.

"I wore it yesterday to the party. You remember it: the

pearl one in the platinum setting. When I got home, I put it on my dressing table along with my necklace and other jewelry. Oh, and my rhinestone hairband and my gloves, of course." Dora's animated face was screwed up in deep concentration.

"So, the last time you saw your ring was yesterday when you took it off." I wasn't sure whether or not this line of questioning would actually be helpful in finding the ring, but it appeared to at least calm my new friend.

"That's right. Golly, you're a regular gumshoe, Ruby!" Dora beamed at me. Her eyes found the girl, who was making herself as small as possible, probably in the hopes of going unnoticed, and her smile slipped. "Scram, Minnie. Why are you always sticking your nose where it doesn't belong? Oh, Ruby, you haven't met Minnie yet, have you? She was staying with our grandmother and just returned. She's my little sister and she's horrible."

Minnie stuck her tongue out in response. I was taken aback by Dora's blatant rudeness. Since Minnie wasn't causing any trouble, I saw no reason to force her to leave, and my heart went out to the girl. However, Dora was clearly annoyed by her very presence and I was reluctant to do anything that would upset my new friend.

"Let's go look at your room. Maybe we'll find something helpful," I suggested as a thundercloud moved back over Dora's face, threatening to burst at any minute.

I could tell she wasn't too keen on the idea, but Dora did get to her feet and lead the way, shoving Minnie out of the way as we passed her. Dora led us down the front hall and up the grand staircase to the second floor. Her room was a large, bright chamber with a big bed, cluttered dressing table, and a small heap of clothes on the floor. It looked the same as it had yesterday and I felt a little disappointed that there wasn't some obvious clue that was readily available for me to find.

Minnie, who had followed us despite Dora's displeasure, took in the mess and clucked her tongue in disapproval.

Dora spun around, irate. "You're not wanted here, Minnie. Breeze!" She made shooing motions at the younger girl until she backed up enough to slam the door shut. We heard a muffled protest from the other side and Dora slumped against the door, grinning evilly. "Do you have any younger sisters, Ruby?"

I shook my head.

"They're the worst. Especially when they're brown-nosing little know-it-alls like Minnie."

While she continued ranting, I made my way to the dressing table and raised my eyebrows. It was covered in cosmetics, bottles of perfumes, and discarded jewelry. Was it possible that the ring was still here?

Before I could say anything, Dora popped her head around my shoulder. "I've looked through all that. I picked up every single thing and put it right back so that the crime scene would be exactly the same for the police." She waved a hand over the clutter. "But, no soap. The ring isn't there."

It would probably be a good idea to go through everything carefully again, despite her assurances. I could only imagine how embarrassed Dora would be if the police were called and the ring turned out to be buried under a pile on the dressing table all along.

I looked the table over, trying to figure out where to dive in. Every inch was covered except for one circular spot right in the center. I was about to ask Dora if she always left that area clean or if something else was missing when the door opened and a young woman in a prim maid's outfit stepped in.

"You!" Dora said, her voice steely. It was a ridiculously dramatic thing to say, but I had to admit that she did it well. Gloria Swanson couldn't have delivered the line better.

The poor maid had clearly been crying. She was so flustered that her hands couldn't seem to decide what they should be doing. "Miss Dora, I didn't steal from you. I'm no thief!"

"Ha! I'm going to tell Charlie to call the fuzz." Dora glided out of the room and I was suddenly aware that she was enjoying this melodrama.

Alone with the maid, I walked to her and put my hand on her shoulder. "Don't worry. We'll find the ring. What's your name?"

"Bessie, miss," she sniffed. "I didn't steal anything, I promise."

If she was acting, it was even more convincing than Dora's earlier performance and I found myself believing her to be innocent. "Don't worry, Bessie. I'll do whatever I can to find out what really happened."

The maid nodded and gave me a shaky smile. "Thank you, miss. I'd better get back to work or the Beaumonts will have a real reason to can me."

I wandered back around the room, trying to notice every detail. Perhaps I'd spot something that would tell me what had really happened. As I scrutinized the mess, I began to consider how tidy the room was underneath the clothes and shoes. The floors were swept, the surfaces free of dust, and the windows sparkled. It was obvious that Bessie cleaned this room regularly. A crumpled peignoir and matching nightgown were slowly making their way off a chair and onto the floor where a pair of delicate slippers with little heels lay. Dora would have taken those off when she dressed this morning.

Another mound proved to be the dress she'd been wearing yesterday at the party. It was joined by the blue silk I'd borrowed, which Dora apparently hadn't bothered to hang up. It was a shame to see such find dresses in such a sorry state. The other heap was underclothes and a pair of Mary Janes.

I walked around the piles again, trying to force them to give up their secrets. Bessie hadn't been in to tidy up after Dora today, that much was clear. It would make sense for the maid to come in once the ladies of the house were up and dressed for the day and collect laundry or straighten the room. That spoke well for Bessie, at least. I wouldn't have been surprised to learn that someone could account for her presence elsewhere since her arrival at the house.

A lovely silver hand mirror lay on the floor, on top of the underclothes, and I clucked my tongue at its rough treatment. This mirror must be a part of a very expensive set. Sure enough, it fit perfectly into the circular space on the dressing table, though the handle hung over the edge.

"No wonder you were knocked down," I chided.

The door burst open and Dora led the way into the room, arms flailing. She was followed by her mother, who was clearly caught up in Dora's dramatic accusations and listening intently. I noticed Minnie sneaking back in behind her mother. Bringing up the rear was Charlie, his gray eyes full of amusement at his sister's antics.

"Dora, my dear," her mother purred, "are you absolutely certain that Bessie took the ring?"

"Yes, there's no doubt in my mind. Who else would have taken it?" Dora's eyes narrowed as she spotted her sister. "Minnie, you didn't pinch my ring, did you? I saw you hoofing out of here when I came out of the john."

"Of course I didn't touch your dopey ring!" Minnie protested loudly. "I don't want any of your gaudy things anyway." Though the covetous look she secretly cast at the dressing table betrayed her.

"I don't think Minnie took it. She's as honest as the day is long," Mrs. Beaumont dismissed Dora's accusation and ran a hand over Minnie's dark curls. "And stop using so much slang, Dora. It's unbecoming of a lady."

My friend's face pinched as though she'd eaten something sour. She opened her mouth to argue further, but her mother held up her hands in surrender.

"I'll call the police and report your missing ring. Does that make you happy?" Mrs. Beaumont looked entirely put out by the morning's events and exhausted by her eldest daughter's dramatics.

Dora's face darkened and she gave her sister a secret pinch where their mother couldn't see. Minnie was ready to howl with displeasure and Charlie smirked at us all from where he leaned against the wall, hands in his pockets. I looked from face to face and decided I needed to step in.

"Excuse me. I think I can help."

Mrs. Beaumont blinked at me in surprise. "Who are you?"

"My name is Ruby Martin and I live next door with Miss Barnes." I watched Dora's mother's lip curl slightly at the reference to Aunt Muriel.

"You remember Ruby, Mother. She was at breakfast yesterday when you told us about Jean Waldeck." Dora appeared annoyed that her mother hadn't bothered to remember her friend.

"Oh, that was you?" Mrs. Beaumont blinked at me

blankly, clearly having no recollection that I'd been in the kitchen at all.

I waited for any further objections to my offer for aid. When none were voiced, I went on. "I have an idea of what might have happened to your ring, Dora. Last night when you came home, did you put your ring into a jewelry box of some sort or did you drop it on the table?"

Dora blinked at me for a moment and the resemblance to her mother was remarkable. "I guess I just dropped it."

I'd expected that, but needed to be sure. "Is it possible that it landed on your hand mirror?"

All eyes darted to the dressing table where the mirror lay. Dora thought for a moment. "I suppose it might have. Oh, wait! Yes, I know it landed on the mirror. After I dropped it, it made a loud sound and I remember looking to make sure that the mirror didn't chip."

"Really, Dora," her mother scolded. "Your father and I gave you that silver mirror and comb set for your sixteenth birthday. It's from Tiffany's! You must learn to be more cautious."

Minnie's chest swelled visibly with superiority as she watched her sister get a telling off.

I turned to the younger girl. "Minnie, when you were in here earlier, were you near the dressing table?"

"Yes," Minnie said slowly, looking between us all.

"Did you knock the mirror off of the table?" I pressed as kindly as I could manage.

Dora's hands went to her hips and her eyes widened threateningly. It was her turn to swell, this time with indignation.

Minnie kicked at the floor. "Yes," she whispered.

"Why, I oughta ..." Dora began, though she stopped with one quelling look from her mother.

For the first time, Charlie joined us. "Say, if Minnie knocked the mirror down and the ring was on it ..."

I nodded. "It would have fallen, too. Depending on how hard Minnie hit it, the ring might even have flown across the room."

Dora gasped in surprise and all five of us bent over as one and began searching. It didn't take long before Charlie reached under a delicate table and lifted the ring from where it was lying, waiting to be discovered.

"Ruby, you are an absolute doll!" Dora threw her arms around me.

"Well done." Mrs. Beaumont offered a doting smile. "It's such a terrible trouble to find good maids. And imagine the fuss and bother if the police had come! I so dislike the idea of having such low people given free rein in my very home."

I felt rather proud of myself for figuring it out, though I didn't want to look too pleased.

"A sleuth right next door." Charlie's pleasant tenor was low and warm. "How lucky for us."

My eyes met his and I couldn't stop a shy smile from following him out of the room. He was tall and broad-shouldered and could have been in the pictures. I remembered how kind he'd been to me at the party and felt my face heating. A moment later, Dora threw her arms around me and squealed.

"You are the cat's pajamas, Ruby, I swear!" Dora pulled back and smiled at me, her dark eyes dancing. "I know! We'll celebrate by going shopping. I'm going to buy you a new outfit."

I opened my mouth to protest. It was too generous. Besides, I couldn't help but think that a better celebration would be an apology to Bessie.

Dora looked to make sure that her family members were out of earshot then leaned forward and grabbed my hand. "Say, I have an idea. I think we should look into Jean's death."

"No," I said quickly. "I'm not going to investigate a murder. Dora, that would be incredibly dangerous."

"Oh, come on. We'll just ask some questions and think things through. Look how well you solved the mystery of my missing ring. You saved Bessie from unfair accusations." She seemed to forget that she had been the accuser. "The police think that Jean's death was an accident but we know the truth."

"No, we don't." I put my hands out in front of me and tried to slow her words. "The only thing we know is that it's unlikely that she was robbed." I didn't want to mention the speculation that Gus and I had made about Jean's death being a murder.

"Don't be such a spoilsport," Dora frowned. "I think you'd be great, and I could be your assistant. I can see the headlines now ..." She stared dreamily into the air.

"No," I said flatly. But, despite my refusal, I began to imagine myself investigating the murder. It's possible that nothing would have come of that silly conversation, but the events of the church supper later that week changed my mind.

CHAPTER FOUR

Aunt Muriel was a very active woman. She and her women's circle from church were busy with a dozen charitable events, planning suppers, knitting and quilting for the poor, and generally running the church's activities. As her niece and fellow spinster, it was assumed that I would naturally join in the group.

After the first meeting, I learned that I was the only person there under the age of 40. While the Port Vernon Methodist Church did boast a number of young families, the tight circle of older women robustly refused entry into their ranks to most anyone in my generation. It made me an anomaly, though I couldn't exactly say that it was a privilege I much appreciated.

After church on Sunday, Aunt Muriel and her ladies served cookies and cider in the fellowship hall. The older women in the group were settled into chairs near the cookie table where they could monitor the children to prevent them from taking more than their fair share of treats. The women who were more active poured coffee, replenished the tray, and generally acted self-importantly.

As the youngest woman in the circle, I was expected to do any and all tedious physical labor including carrying the trays and pitchers back and forth to the small kitchen. When Mrs. Owens needed the coffee pot refilled, I was expected to go to the pump in the small churchyard and work the icy handle until it belched forth water, protesting with horrific creaks all the while.

So I wasn't at all surprised when, the day after I cleared up the matter of Dora's lost ring, Aunt Muriel announced that we would spend the day cooking a supper at the church in order to raise funds to repair the old church bells. It wasn't at all how I would have chosen to spend the day, but I understood that it wasn't optional.

We walked the five blocks to the church, wrapped up against the biting wind, Aunt Muriel nattering away the entire time.

I mostly ignored her complaints of how young people couldn't handle the cold like her generation could. In fact, I was so busy thinking about how much I missed my family that I didn't notice when she switched to a new topic. My mind lurched back to what she was saying when she mentioned the problems they were having at church.

"Louise Wick has been impossible since the latest group of people got sick after our fish fry."

I almost tripped as I tried to decide if I'd heard her right. "I'm sorry, Aunt Muriel, what did you say? People at church have been sick?"

She looked at me over the top of her spectacles. "That's what I said. Were you wool gathering instead of paying attention?"

I shrugged, feeling like a little girl caught daydreaming

at school. "You said 'the latest group.' Does that mean that many people have been ill? This has happened before?"

"It's not our fault." She was instantly defensive. "I suppose a stomach illness of some sort has been passing around the community."

"Other people in town have reported being sick then?" I pressed.

"No one has said so to me," she admitted.

"How many times has this happened?"

"Four people reported being sick after the fish fry. Five after the stew supper. I believe it was three after the potluck in September. That's how I know that it isn't our cooking that is the problem."

I screwed up my face. "I don't understand. What does that prove?"

Aunt Muriel looked positively imperial as she said, "The women's circle didn't provide the food for the potluck. Everyone cooked at home. In fact, we thought it would be wise to let the younger generation do the work for a change and we only provided beverages and desserts from the bakery." She snorted with derision. "It was an expense I didn't approve of, but Ida Mills donated everything, so my word didn't mean much. And once Louise Wick was put in charge of the committee, it would be like stopping a rampaging rhino."

I'd stopped paying attention to my aunt's criticisms. People getting sick was strange, and my mind was whirling. People were getting sick to their stomachs after eating at the church. Was it an odd coincidence? Was there a particularly rich dish that didn't agree with most people?

Mrs. Wick was very put out about the problem. As head of the women's circle, she took the illnesses as a personal insult. Once we arrived at the church and donned our aprons, we were treated to a lecture on food preparation safety.

"We aren't going to take any chances," Mrs. Wick summarized. "Clean hands, clean utensils."

I was soon left to my own devices. Each woman had a job and knew it well. The entire women's circle worked together remarkably well. The older women helped where they could and were given simple jobs. Mrs. Davenport oversaw the spreading of tablecloths and setting up of the serving tables. I was assigned to her supervision and was soon sweating as I wrestled chairs down from their stacks and tucked them under the tables. Several women who were so old that they were more wrinkles than anything else were busy wrapping silverware with paper napkins. They clucked and chuckled and general spoke too loudly and misheard each other.

Pastor Mason entered the room and cheerfully surveyed us all. I was just putting the last of the chairs out when he clapped a fatherly hand on my shoulder.

"We're glad for your help, Ruby," he said in his booming voice. "I imagine that you've had a great deal of practice helping at these sorts of events."

I wiped a hand across my forehead and smiled. "You're right about that. My brother and I spent more time at church than at home when Father's church had big events." I chewed my lip for a moment and made up my mind. "Pastor Mason, may I ask you a few questions about the recent illnesses?"

He tucked his thumbs into vest pockets and frowned. "They are certainly mysterious. I can't figure out if they are due to something happening here at the church or just an odd coincidence."

"Has anyone investigated them?"

"No, we didn't think it was a matter for the police. A few cases of undercooked food wouldn't concern them."

"If it was badly cooked fish," I mused, "wouldn't more people have been sick? Only four cases doesn't seem to suggest that there was something wrong with how they were cooked."

Pastor Mason considered this. "Perhaps if it was just one batch in the skillet, it might have only affected a few people."

I nodded slowly. "But what about the stew? It would have been one big pot, wouldn't it?"

"Yes, you're right there. Though the potluck supper could have been one dish."

"Who was it that was affected? Was it just children or the elderly? Was it people who are typically weaker or was it strong, healthy people?"

He scratched his chin and his eyes roamed the room as though remembering the layout of his parishioners. He pointed a thick finger at a table in the corner and nodded to himself. "Yes, I remember now. It was the Knight family at the potluck. We didn't think anything of it since they were all in the same family. They might have eaten something bad at home."

That news made me frown. It would be disappointing to have the illnesses explained away so easily. I shook my head at that thought. Apparently, the mystery at the Beaumont's and Jean Waldeck's death had made me hungry for more problems to unravel.

"However, after the stew supper, we were all concerned because Joe Stephens, Morris Hopkins, and the three Davis sisters were sick." His finger moved to a table across the way, closer to the kitchen.

I cocked my head and narrowed my eyes. "All of them sat at the same table?"

He seemed a little surprised. "Now that you mention it, yes, I believe they did share a table. How very odd."

"What about the four at the fish fry? Did they sit together?"

"It was Mr. and Mrs. Dorchester, Sylvester Young, and Miss Turner who were ill. Sylvester sat at a table near them, but not at their table. It was just the three others sitting there." He pointed to a spot near the door to the hallway.

I wasn't sure just yet what this all meant.

"Ruby, come help carry the punch bowl," Aunt Muriel barked at me from the kitchen door.

I thanked the pastor and hurried off to do my aunt's bidding. Thoughts of the strange food poisoning were pushed away as I helped Mrs. Davenport carry stacks of plates from the cupboard in the hallway.

"Did you hear about the death of that girl?" she asked me with an air of one who knew something she was dying to share.

"Jean Waldeck?" I clarified. "I read about it in the paper. Did you know her?"

"Oh, yes," Mrs. Davenport nodded smugly. "Before I married Mr. Davenport, I was a teacher in the local school and Jean was in my class."

This could hardly be information that would help me solve the case. Still, I feigned interest and Mrs. Davenport continued talking as she led the way back into the fellowship hall.

"She was a terrible student. Her brother, Gordon, was even worse. No matter how many times I told her mother that the children needed discipline at home, she never listened. Of course, she was working two jobs at the time and was never home." Mrs. Davenport moved the stack of plates I deposited on the table and then turned to go for another armload of dishes.

"Were you surprised to hear that Jean died?" I pried.

"Just between you and me, I heard that she was involved with a gangster. You know that her brother is in a sanatorium because he took," she glanced around and then hissed, "*drugs.*"

I widened my eyes, trying to look properly shocked at this revelation.

She nodded at me, apparently satisfied with my reaction. "I've always said this is the sort of thing that happens when a mother isn't at home to care for her children."

It wasn't the last I heard about Jean. Everyone was talking about the poor girl. Old Mrs. Worth had been Jean's mother's Sunday school teacher back before the turn of the century and told me in her crackly voice that the girl had never learned to say the Lord's Prayer correctly. Mrs. Owens had once had to chase the Waldeck children out of her garden on more than one occasion. Mrs. Allen reported seeing Jean rouging her knees with her stockings rolled down.

No one had anything good to say about Jean and I felt sorry for her. She'd had a brother whose health had been ruined by drug use, a mother who had to work two jobs to care for her family, and a boyfriend who wasn't very nice. What a sad legacy to leave behind.

The men arrived with the pig that they'd cooked all day and the women pulled out their pies, cornbread, baked beans, and dozens of ears of boiled corn on the cob. People began to arrive, and I was busy running everywhere until Mrs. Wick suggested I help Mrs. Ida Mills.

Mrs. Mills sat at the table inside the door, collecting

money. As the treasurer of the women's circle and, I learned, of the entire church, she watched the till with an eagle eye. Aunt Muriel had told me that the woman was a wealthy widow and had helped her husband with their business. The way Aunt Muriel spoke of Mrs. Mills made me believe that the two ladies were no more than cordial. I don't think my aunt trusted anyone who was too wealthy.

As I sat next to Mrs. Mills, I marveled at her ability to handle the money like a banker and still manage to carry on a conversation fluidly.

"How do you like living with your aunt?" she asked as she dropped a quarter into the till and pulled up a nickel in change.

"She's been very generous to let me move in with her," I responded as politely as possible.

Mrs. Mills eyed me knowingly. "I've known Muriel Barnes for forty years. We went to school together when we were girls. She's as tight as a girdle on a hippopotamus."

I giggled behind my hand, feeling disloyal to my aunt even as I did it.

"There's a dime in change," Mrs. Mills said to the next customer. To me, she said, "If Muriel Barnes ever got a dollar bill in her wallet, it would grow ingrown hairs before she spent it."

A snort escaped me as I tried not to laugh too loudly. Mrs. Mills winked at me and I excused myself. While the last thing I wanted was to insult my aunt, it was really wonderful to have someone understand what life with her was like.

I was hoping to find something else to do to pass the time when Mrs. Wick rounded the corner, all in a dither. She put her hand on my arm and panted for a moment.

"Oh, dear," Mrs. Wick said breathlessly, putting her

other hand to her heaving bosom. "Mrs. Worth was assigned to refill the salt and pepper shakers and forgot to put them on the tables. Please, Ruby, can you hurry and put them out? I don't want to think what would happen if we didn't have salt available for the pastor."

I resisted rolling my eyes and hurried into the kitchen. It hardly seemed like the disaster Mrs. Wick was making it out to be, but I had too much experience with my own mother and church events to say anything to the worried Mrs. Wick as she coordinated the supper. Besides, Mrs. Worth was in her 80s and was so frail that she was unsteady even with the help of the cane. She was always given the job of refilling the salt and pepper shakers because it was one of the simplest duties. The poor old dear would complete her job and then find a seat and nod off, snoring quietly. Putting the shakers out would have been an easy task to overlook. I told Mrs. Wick that I'd take care of it and went to the kitchen to gather up the shakers.

As I moved around the room, putting a pair on each table, it seemed as though everyone was talking about Jean's death. It was big news, I realized, even in a town as big as Port Vernon. Of course, most people had known Jean since she'd been born and raised right here. Everyone knew her or her family. No one seemed to suspect that her death had been a murder and not a robbery gone wrong. Many people clucked their tongues over the foolishness of going for a walk so late, but they seemed generally unsurprised that such a thing had happened to a girl like Jean.

It was a relief to shoo everyone away and clean up. Thankfully, the men lent a hand with putting away tables and chairs and some of the younger women were allowed to wash dishes while their children played noisily, annoying the older women.

Aunt Muriel and I stumbled home and both of us went gratefully to bed before nine o'clock. We arose early the next morning and went about our chores with my aunt rehashing the entire event and criticizing everyone.

When Aunt Muriel realized she'd forgotten her best pan at the church, I gladly volunteered to walk over and fetch it for her. It was a lovely break from my aunt's sour words and I enjoyed the quiet, though my mind jumped between the mystery of Jean's death and the mystery of the poisoned parishioners as I strolled along.

The church was unlocked and I went inside quietly. Aunt Muriel's dish was sitting on the counter, clean and dried. I picked it up and was about to leave when Pastor Mason came out of his study, his face red.

"Oh, hello, Ruby," he said, clearly flustered.

"Is something wrong, Pastor Mason?" I asked.

He sighed. "I hate to say it, but there is. Do you remember what we spoke about yesterday?" He waited for my nod. "I just received word that another person has been ill. Mrs. Dean and her son, Clarence, were up all night. I don't know what we're going to do. We simply can't continue to have suppers like this if someone is going to be sick every time."

I noted his coat and the small pouch in his hand. "Are you going somewhere?"

Pastor Mason looked down at the pouch. "I was going to the bank to deposit the money we took in last night when I received word about the Deans. I should visit them after I go to the bank."

The front door opened and in came a windblown young girl. "Pastor Mason, Mama asked if you could come."

"What's wrong, Lizzie?" he asked.

The little girl pushed strands of hair out of her face with mittened hands. "Papa has been sick and can't go to work today. Mama wants you to visit and pray for him."

The pastor and I exchanged a worried look. This was a possible third case.

"Did Lizzie's family sit with the Deans?" I inquired.

Pastor Mason closed his eyes as he remembered. "Yes, I believe they did. Lizzie, did you sit with Mr. and Mrs. Dean last night?"

"I played with Clarence," she nodded.

"Tell your mother I'll be by as soon as I can."

The little girl turned and shoved open the door as Pastor Mason turned to me. "Ruby, would you mind taking this money to First Bank on Main Street? The deposit slip is inside. Mrs. Mills put everything in order last night before she left."

"Of course." I smiled at him, trying to look reassuring and competent.

I felt a little silly walking into the bank with Aunt Muriel's pan, but I was glad to be able to help Pastor Mason. It was so strange that a small group of people was getting sick after each event. What in the world was happening? It hardly seemed likely that someone was doing something nefarious, but it was difficult to say for certain.

The teller called me forward and I handed over the pouch, explaining that I was running an errand for the church. The man behind the iron grate opened the bag and began to count out the stack of bills.

Still distracted by my thoughts, it took me a few minutes before I noticed just how big that stack was. I calculated in my mind. Each meal had cost a dime a piece and there had been no more than 100 people in the fellowship hall. How could Pastor Mason be depositing more than two hundred dollars into the church's account?

I blinked at the money. Surely the week's offerings hadn't been so much. I knew that Dad rarely had more than five dollars a week in the collection plate. However, there wasn't really anything wrong, and so I accepted the teller's receipt and put it into the bag without saying a word.

On the walk back home, I bit my lip and tried to think of reasons why there would be so much money. Perhaps someone had made a very generous donation. Possibly, Pastor Mason hadn't deposited money in a very long time. Would Mrs. Mills have had a reason to allow that? From the way she'd handled the payments last night, I'd gotten the impression that she was capable and meticulous.

As I arrived home, I sighed and shook my head. I never would have guessed that moving to Aunt Muriel's would have produced so many mysteries. Dora's words about investigating Jean's death wouldn't leave me alone. The mystery at church was the third I'd encountered since coming here. Was solving mysteries some sort of destiny I'd never before imagined?

Despite my insistence that a new outfit was unnecessary and far too generous, Dora was not to be dissuaded. That was how I found myself at Howard's Department store the very next day, where it became immediately obvious that my new friend was an expert when it came to shopping for clothes.

The salesgirls perked up at the sight of Dora Beaumont sailing through the door. I thought she looked remarkably like Clara Bow with her red cupid's bow mouth and short, dark bob, as she took charge of everyone within earshot. We were soon seated in a private back room, being served tea and delicate finger sandwiches. Models strutted out, showing us how the newest fashions looked on a real person.

I observed the entire thing with wide eyes. Most of my clothes came from missionary barrels and boasted at least one previous owner. Dora, on the other hand, took it all in stride, calling out orders to the young women who stopped and turned at her every command.

"What do you think of silk, Ruby?" she asked, giving a keen eye to the twirling models and completely missing my awe. "I know it's November, but silk crepe romaine is so pretty."

Swallowing my sandwich, I stammered, "I doubt I'll get much chance to wear silk."

My new friend turned shocked eyes on me. "Whatever do you mean? Of course you'll have chances to wear silk! We'll get out our glad rags at least once a week! You don't think that I don't know how to show a newcomer a good time, do you? I don't mind lending you my things, but we aren't the same size and you simply have to have a dress that was made after they signed the Treaty of Versailles." She watched me sit there, trying to think of something to say, before patting my knee. "Just you trust old Auntie Dora. Oh, look at that one!"

I had to put away my qualms and focus on the task at hand. She immediately began trying to convince me that I should let her buy me a lovely dress with a sheer georgette overlay. If she was really going to buy me a new dress, however, I was determined that it be something I would get a great deal of wear out of.

We haggled back and forth and finally agreed upon a

sensible wool dress. The fabric had a slight sheen to it, which pleased Dora, and was the sort of thing I could wear to church, which pleased me. I was ordered to take off my current brown dress in order to get fitted for the new one.

Once Dora saw the state of my underclothes, she immediately ordered the salesgirl to add a new brassiere, underpants, and slip to our order. I couldn't dissuade Dora from purchasing silk stockings, though my father always said they were extravagant when wool stockings were so much more practical and modest.

"You're so lucky that you have such a good figure," she sighed. "You were made to wear the modern styles. I, on the other hand, will never be as straight up and down. Having a front like mine is the worst thing I can possibly imagine."

I resisted the urge to roll my eyes at her. Dora was four inches shorter than I was and despite her girdle and corset, couldn't force her curvaceous self into the ideal flapper silhouette. After seeing her mother's build, I knew she was in for a lifetime of disappointment if that was a dream she kept chasing.

Unfortunately, I was completely lacking when it came to feminine curves. While it was fashionable, it also made me feel like I looked 12 years old. Only 20 years ago, Dora's figure would have been the enviable one and mine, pitiable. I considered pointing this out but knew that it wouldn't make much difference to my friend. She was able to buy just about everything else that she wanted and couldn't quite reconcile the fact that she couldn't change this, no matter how much money she had.

By the time we were looking at shoes, it stopped being a matter of whether or not Dora would buy me shoes and became whether or not I could convince her to let me buy loafers instead of Mary Janes.

It was several hours later when we stepped out on the street, our arms laden with packages. The new navy blue wool dress with contrasting embroidery on the cuffs and pockets was in one box. My new underclothes were in another. The tan calfskin lace-up shoes with a low heel were already on my feet and my new leaf-green cloche covered my blonde hair. Even though my coat was out-of-date, I was sure that everyone was admiring me.

"I don't know how to thank you," I said for the tenth time. "I've never had new clothes from a store before."

"That is a tragedy," Dora said seriously. "I can't imagine how awful your life has been until now."

I laughed. "It hasn't been awful. We just never had money for new things. Besides, my parents would rather spend their money helping those in need." I didn't mention that Dad would have balked at the idea of his daughter actually enjoying shopping at a department store.

"I think that being a minister's daughter is the most awful thing that could happen to a person." Dora looked into my eyes and squeezed my hand. "I'm terribly glad that we are going to be friends. I can pull you from the pit of despair that your life has been until now."

I hid my grin.

"Let's get a soda," Dora suggested.

"Oh," I said, embarrassed once again. "Gee, Dora, I can't."

"Do you have to get home to your aunt?" she asked.

"It's not that." I felt like a heel. I only had a dollar to my name and simply couldn't spend it on something as frivolous as a soda.

Dora grabbed my arm and pulled me to a stop. She put her fists on her hips and looked up at me fiercely. "Let's get one thing straight, Ruby Martin. We aren't going to have a fight every time I want to do something that costs money."

"I don't want to be your charity case." I kicked at the ground, remembered my new shoes, and checked to make sure I hadn't scuffed them. "You can't pay for everything."

"Whyever not?" Dora's eyes softened. "I have an idea. What if you work as my secretary a few hours a week? You can handle my correspondence and phone calls and such. In return, I'll pick up the check whenever we go out."

"Aunt Muriel would be sure to let me spend more time with you if she knew it was my job," I mused, excitement stirring. "It's a great idea, Dora. Thank you."

She preened. "I know!" Then she slipped her arm under mine, and the two of us headed off towards the drugstore, laughing.

We'd no sooner ordered our sodas from the soda jerk at the counter than the door opened and we both turned to look as Gus came strolling in.

"Well, hello there," Dora whistled. "What a sheik! And he's such a good dancer, too."

I swallowed hard. Gus' cheeks were flushed with cold and he was wearing a rough jacket that couldn't be much defense against the wind. The effect was that of a sturdy young man who wasn't overly bothered by things like cold weather. Much to my chagrin, he was every bit as good-looking as I'd been trying to convince myself I'd misremembered.

He looked over a display before feeling our eyes on us and glancing our way. Immediately, he put down the bottle he'd been examining and came our way.

"Imagine running into you two here," he said to me.

"Join us," Dora offered, and came to sit next to me in the booth.

"I don't mind if I do," Gus said with a grin and slid across from us. "Say, Ruby, I was thinking over what you said the other day when we were walking. I have a friend who works at the docks. He covers a lot of night shifts. What do you say I ask him if he knows anything about Louis Hardy?"

I would have refused just a few days ago. Asking questions about a drug smuggler was sure to be dangerous. Yet mysteries kept finding me, and I had to admit that I was enjoying it. Surely there could be no harm in asking questions about Jean's death. We wouldn't get too close, and we would turn anything we found over to the police right away.

"I think that's a good idea," I said with a nod.

Dora sat up straighter in her seat. "Are we going to investigate?"

"Carefully," I amended quickly. "We'll be extremely careful and not keep anything from the police."

Dora and Gus exchanged an excited grin and I found myself joining in.

CHAPTER FIVE

O ver the next few days, my life in Port Vernon took on a pattern. I got up early, dressed, and tidied my room. Then I headed downstairs to help Aunt Muriel fix breakfast. She always had a few chores to criticize me through before I was allowed to head off to the Beaumonts. Dora would put me to work as her secretary, which meant that I was required to take on tasks that I doubted any secretary had ever been asked to do such as piecing together the torn fragments of a photo she'd ripped apart after a long night of drinking.

Dora derived great pleasure from dropping by my aunt's house and saying provocative things that made Aunt Muriel's eyebrows confer with her hairline. During those visits, my aunt would sniff in response to anything that Dora said of which she disapproved. And since Aunt Muriel hated flappers, slang, and gossip (or so she said), it often sounded as though she had a bad head cold.

"I brought you my second best pearls," Dora announced as she burst through the door one afternoon in early December. "I thought you'd need them for our annual Christmas party."

I turned to her, smiling in relief at the interruption. Aunt Muriel had decided that, as a future spinster, it was important that I learn how to knit. Apparently, knitting was especially good for women like us because it could benefit the poor, make bandages for soldiers in times of war, and create inexpensive gifts for loved ones.

My aunt sniffed loudly, her eyes never leaving her knitting.

"Hello, Miss Barnes," Dora simpered, "lovely to see you today. That color of brown looks absolutely divine on you."

I hid my smile behind my hand. "I didn't realize I was expected to attend the Beaumont Christmas party."

"Of course you'll be there! I'll need your help all day. Mother is always swimming in work and we'll both have to lend both hands to get everything finished on time." She winked at me before sighing dramatically. "You can't imagine how hard it is to oversee the servants."

We escaped upstairs and collapsed on my bed in a fit of giggles.

"You shouldn't egg Aunt Muriel on like that! I thought steam would start coming out of her ears."

"It's good for her," Dora dismissed my halfhearted admonition.

We hadn't settled down for long before a knock sounded at the front door. Aunt Muriel's footsteps could be heard all the way upstairs as she stomped to the foyer. The door creaked open and then we could hear her talking with a man.

"Who could that be?" I wondered. "No man ever comes to the door unless he's delivering something and then he always uses the kitchen door."

"Maybe she's got a long-lost lover who's finally found her." Dora waggled her eyebrows at me and we giggled some more.

The sound of my aunt's steps sobered us as she came to the top of the stairs and announced, "Ruby, there's a young man to see you."

We instantly sobered. A young man to see me? Other than Charlie, I couldn't imagine who it would be. Dora and I dashed to the mirror to check our hair before scampering down the hall, down the stairs, and coming to a stop at the door.

"Oh, it's you," Dora said, disappointed, I'm sure, that it wasn't some dashing daddy.

I, on the other hand, felt my heart race at the sight of Gus Jones leaning against the door jamb.

"Hello to you, too," he smirked at Dora.

"Gus, what are you doing here?" I asked.

He shot my aunt a meaningful look and said carefully, "I found that book you were asking me about."

Book? What book? My mind scrambled as I tried to figure out what he was saying. Then my eyes widened as I cottoned on. "Oh, you did? Where did you find it?"

Gus pushed his hands into his pockets and rocked back on his heels. His voice was far too innocent as he announced, "It's in a shop downtown. If you're not busy, now would be a good time to go and look at it. I promised the shopkeeper I'd be back shortly and he's holding it for us, but we'll have to hurry."

"What a good idea," I said quickly, before either Dora or Aunt Muriel could butt in. "Let me get my coat and purse."

"Swell," Gus answered as he came inside to wait, shutting the door behind him and giving the front hall an appraising glance.

I ran upstairs to fetch my purse and Aunt Muriel followed me.

"Why are you continuing to have contact with that young man?" she hissed. "I doubt your parents would approve of you spending time with someone like him."

"I ran into Gus a few weeks back and he was kind enough to walk me home. We talked about ... books and I mentioned, er, one that I couldn't find. He said he knew someone to ask and that he'd let me know if he learned anything." My conscience squirmed at the fib, but my irritation with my aunt silenced it.

"Besides, Aunt Muriel," I soothed, "Dora will be coming with me. Isn't it important for us to be kind to all people?"

The sour look on her face disagreed plainly, though she didn't say anything as I hurried back downstairs.

"What's really going on?" Dora asked as soon as we were out of earshot of the house.

"Remember when I said I'd talk to my friend who works at the docks? Well, he's agreed to let us ask him some questions," Gus explained.

My curiosity couldn't be contained any longer. "Did you find out anything?"

"I don't know anything for certain, so don't get your hopes up too high," he cautioned. I nodded impatiently and he went on. "This fellow has been covering the nightshift lately and mentioned seeing Hardy's boat coming in and out of port."

"Does that mean anything?" Dora asked hopefully.

Gus shrugged, "Maybe yes, maybe no. We'll have to see what else he knows."

My toes were numb by the time we pushed into the diner where Gus had arranged for us to meet his friend,

Liam. All four of us settled into a booth and Dora ordered egg creams for both of us.

"Liam, this is that dame I was telling you about." Gus jabbed his thumb at me.

Liam eyed me warily before nodding slightly. His worn newsboy cap, faded work shirt, and rough hands all bespoke a life of hard labor.

"Tell Ruby what you were telling me," Gus directed. "About Louis Hardy and the ship."

Liam swallowed the bite of sandwich he'd been chewing before saying, "You know Hardy's a smuggler, right?"

I nodded again. "He smuggles alcohol from Canada."

Liam glanced around shiftily. "Everyone knows that hooch comes over Lake Huron. Even the bulls know about it, though they take bribes to look the other way. But I've started hearing that other things are coming over that way."

"Other things?" Dora asked, her voice too loud. "What else are they bringing over?"

Liam and Gus both cringed and glanced around to see if anyone was listening. I was struck at the similarity between the two men and another light bulb of understanding about Gus's life clicked on. He was from this same hardworking, hard-knock side of town.

"I don't know for sure, but some say China white, some say dope, some say people."

I sucked in a long breath. If Louis was bringing drugs or illegal aliens over the border, he could be in serious trouble. And if Jean was connected to Louis, she would have been right in the path of that trouble. It was no longer shocking that she had been killed if she associated with people who were in such a dangerous business.

"How can we find out for certain if Louis is smuggling those things?" I asked.

Liam shook his head vehemently. "Keep your nose out of it, sister. You don't mess around with gangsters."

"Gangsters?" Dora cried, and this time all three of us cringed.

"Come on, Liam, you've got to tell her about the boat," Gus pressed.

Looking entirely unhappy, Liam went on, "I saw Louis Hardy coming in after dark on the *Baker's Dozen* three nights last week when I was working the graveyard shift. He and his men unloaded more than twenty crates and took them off to a warehouse."

My heart picked up its pace. "What warehouse?"

"I didn't see." Liam drank down the rest of his soda. "I even checked the warehouse list, but there isn't anything in his name."

I sat back against the seat, disappointed. It would have been too easy to go to the police and tell them where to check for Hardy's illegal goods. Once they arrested him for smuggling drugs, they could ask him about Jean's death.

"Thanks," Gus said as Liam slid out of the booth and got to his feet. "We'll get your check."

Liam nodded and the two shook hands before Liam shrugged into his coat and loped out the door.

"Who's getting his check?" Dora groused. "I know you sure don't plan on paying for this, Gus Jones."

Gus shot her a cheeky grin. "I figured you'd pony up the clams, princess."

"Let's get out of here, Ruby," she sniffed. "I want to go to the beauty parlor to have my hair set for the Christmas party."

We all tromped to the cash register where Dora did, in fact, pay the bill.

Out on the sidewalk, I turned to Gus, not sure what to say next.

"Thanks for letting me talk to Liam," I said lamely.

"One more clue," Gus winked. "I'll keep putting out bait and see if we catch anything else. See you, cookie."

Dora took my elbow and we hurried off in the other direction. I managed a brief glance over my shoulder as we turned the corner, but Gus had disappeared. Disappointed, I dragged my attention back to Dora's chatter.

CHAPTER SIX

The Beaumont's Christmas party was the most glamorous thing I'd ever seen. The house was transformed with shimmering decorations, strings of lights, and vase after vase of flowers. Extra hired hands carried trays with delicate canapés and flutes of champagne. A real four-piece string ensemble played tasteful music in the dining room and the best of the best of Port Vernon society appeared, wearing the latest fashions.

I spent the evening trailing behind Dora and trying not to goggle at everything. Charlie asked me to dance several times and I enjoyed having such a good dance partner. All said, I had a nice time, though I couldn't reconcile the fact that so much illegal alcohol was being served right out in the open. Dora pointed out the mayor and the chief of police who were drinking at the bar. It left me feeling wrongfooted and I wasn't sorry to eventually escape the festivities and head across the backyard to Aunt Muriel's simpler abode.

"I wish we knew what the police know about Jean's death," I sighed the next day. Thanks to Dora's attitude about church, I hadn't mentioned anything about the strange happenings there. I hoped that focusing on Jean's death would get my mind off of poison and the large bank deposit.

Dora was lying on her stomach on her bed, feet in the air, reading the latest copy of *Photoplay* magazine. She slowly lowered it to the bed and gave me a critical stare. "Have you thought of something else we can do to investigate?"

"Not really. I keep going over what we know to see if I can make sense of it." I pointed the nail file I'd been using at her. "We know that Jean wasn't just out for a leisurely stroll the night she was killed. She had a dangerous boyfriend, and she didn't have anything worth stealing. Furthermore, she was strangled, which isn't usually the way that thieves kill their victims. I wish I knew whether or not the police know any of those things."

"Ruby, you can't tell the police that we were at that party."

"Why not? It was weeks ago. I doubt they'll arrest you for a little gin."

Dora's face was suddenly very secretive. My heart began pounding. "Dora, what else happened at that party?"

She rolled her eyes and slowly got to her knees. "Now, before you start acting like a Mrs. Grundy and lecturing me for an hour, remember that I didn't do anything. I just ... might have ... seen someone buying something illegal."

I rolled that around in my mind. "You saw someone buy something illegal. Something other than alcohol?"

"I might have," Dora hedged, refusing to make eye contact.

"All right." I tried to make sense of why this mattered. "What happened?"

My friend fiddled with her skirt for a few moments

before she began. "After you left, I had to iron my shoelaces, so I went in search of a bathroom. It turns out that the house didn't have indoor plumbing, so I had to the outhouse. Which, I must say, was horrifying. I don't know how our ancestors survived before indoor toilets came around."

"Dora, you're getting off topic."

"Okay, okay," she sighed. "While I was out back I saw a certain fellow we both know handing money over to Louis Hardy. And then Louis gave him something back."

Some fellow we both knew? I chewed my lip. Did she mean Charlie? Or Gus? Or some other young man she'd introduced me to who I couldn't remember? It took a minute before I understood what she was reluctant to say.

"Dora, do you mean that you saw someone buying drugs from Louis Hardy?"

Her eyes met mine and she nodded.

I was out of the chair and clambering onto the bed in the next instant. "Who did you see buying drugs from Louis Hardy? Was it Charlie?" My voice dropped to a whisper.

Please don't let it be Gus, my heart prayed frantically.

Dora pursed her lips and looked away. Finally, she said, "Yes, it was Charlie. But he was only buying reefer, which is practically the same thing as tobacco."

I sat back, both relieved and shocked. I liked Dora's brother. As glad as I was that it hadn't been Gus buying drugs, I didn't want Charlie to be hurt by them either.

"I didn't want to tell you before," Dora pleaded. "I didn't want you thinking that Charlie is some sort of addict or something. He only uses a little when he's at parties. Most of the boys in his group do. Anyway, that's the real reason that you can't say anything to the police. It's one thing to be arrested for having a little hooch. If the police find out that he's been buying drugs, he'll lose any chance he's got at having a good future."

It was odd to see Dora looking serious. She liked to be melodramatic, but rarely did she show the real girl hiding behind the pretense of drinking and dancing and making people love her.

My brain was still formulating a response when she abruptly changed the subject. "I have the most darb idea! Let's go down to Mabel's Café. That's where all the peepers go after their shifts. I'll bet we could find a young policeman, charm him, and learn what he knows about the case. Oh, Ruby, it'll be the berries!"

I knew she was dodging further discussion of Charlie's bad habits and didn't have the heart to go back to it. So I pulled on my own coat and followed her down the stairs and out the door.

She kept up a steady stream of idle conversation about movie stars and fashions all the way to the café. By the time we blew through the door of Mabel's Café, the perky mask was firmly back in place and Dora was every inch the bubbleheaded socialite she worked so hard to make people believe she was.

But when we stepped into the café, Dora fell silent and we both took in the sight of more than a dozen police officers sitting, lounging, eating, and drinking. They hardly looked up when we stepped through the door.

I had no idea what to do next. My brain completely forgot the reason we were there as I looked around at all the uniformed strangers. Dora, however, had no such qualms. She walked jauntily up to the counter and ordered two cups of coffee and a plate of doughnuts. Then she leaned casually as she waited for our order to be filled, nonchalantly examining each and every man in the café. All of her years of interacting with men seemed to be paying off as my friend applied her expertise to discerning which police officer would be most likely to help us.

"I know just the one," she whispered to me. We picked up our mugs and plate and began to weave our way through the tables.

Since there were several empty booths and a few open tables, I had no choice but to follow Dora until she stopped at whatever target she'd settled on. When she stopped at a little table and began to take off her coat while studiously avoiding the appreciative glances sent her way, I understood her plan. Next to our table was a booth with three younger-looking constables. All three wore the dark blue suits with shiny gold buttons, sported similar short haircuts, and were taking a lot of notice of the two young ladies who were making themselves comfortable at the next table over. Dora had chosen wisely, I decided.

"Golly, Ruby, I was just so scared," she began as soon as we sat down.

I blinked at her, unsure what my lines were in this drama that she was inventing as she went along.

With a hand on her bosom, she gulped dramatically. "Thank goodness we were close to Mabel's where we'd be safe with so many police officers."

"Pardon me, but I couldn't help overhearing," one of the young policemen interjected. "Can we be of service?"

Faster than you'd have thought possible, the three young men had slid out of their booth and were pulling up chairs at our table. Dora smiled weakly at them all and their chests swelled. I had to hide my snicker with my coffee cup. These fellows were violins and Dora was playing each and every one of them.

"I'm Officer Grey," said the handsome one with big ears. "This is Officer Reilly and Officer Peterson."

"Dora Beaumont," she purred, holding up a dainty hand to clasp each man's in turn. "This is my dear friend, Ruby Martin."

"What happened out there, Miss Beaumont?" Officer Peterson was small and wiry, with a gap-toothed grin that made it hard to take him seriously.

"An unsavory fellow was trying to get us to shell out a few clams. We refused, and he started following us. As soon as we came in here, he took off the other way." Dora smiled shyly. "Thank goodness all of you were here to scare him off."

"Would you like us to see you home?" Officer Reilly was redhaired, freckled, and also the size of a bull.

"Oh, that's so kind of you," purred my friend, "but I'm sure he's gone now. You're welcome to stay at our table with us. We simply adore men in blue, don't we, Ruby, dear?"

I kicked her under the table, hoping she'd stop laying it on so thick. The police officers, however, all preened and grinned.

"I'll bet you three have been in all kinds of danger over the years, haven't you?" Dora's wide eyes and pretty red lips charmed each one of the constables. In no time, they were each trying to outdo each other with stories of their bravery. Gasping and giggling at all the right moments, Dora played her part perfectly. There was little for me to do but try and keep up with her.

Finally, she slid in the question we'd come to ask. Looking suddenly sad, she said, "A friend of mine was killed not too long ago. We've been hoping to hear that her murderer has been caught, but so far there's been no word.

It's just too, too sad to think that Jean's killer might get away."

"Jean Waldeck?" Officer Reilly asked. "Ted here's been on that case since the beginning."

Our eyes, now big because we were anxiously awaiting the details that might come spilling forth, swung to Officer Grey.

"The papers said that it was a robbery gone wrong," he hedged. "There isn't much chance that we'll find him unless he strikes again."

I had a hunch that Ted Grey knew more than he was sharing. It was time for me to channel my inner Hercule Poirot. "Come now, officer, everyone knew that Jean was involved with Louis Hardy. It's too much of a coincidence to believe that a girl dating a known criminal just happened to be killed in a random robbery."

All three policemen appraised me as though they were noticing me for the first time.

"That's what Sergeant Sandercock was saying," Peterson put in. "I overheard him saying that they found her purse in a trashcan in the alley where they found her body and it still had ten dollars in it."

I sat up straighter. "They did?"

Officer Grey's eyes narrowed. "You're awfully interested in this investigation, Miss Martin."

"I don't want a killer to go free," I answered honestly. "It seemed odd to me that it could be a robbery gone wrong. Besides, why would a young woman be out for a stroll by herself that late at night?"

"And in her glad rags," Dora added. Instantly, her eyes bugged. She hadn't meant to give that detail away.

"What do you mean?" Grey was intrigued.

Dora's eyes darted around as though she was trying to find a way out of the café.

I put a hand on her leg under the table and said, "We saw the picture of her body in the paper and noticed that she was wearing pearls and a party dress. If she'd been out for a walk, she would have been wearing an everyday dress that was much warmer." I shot Dora a look. "We thought she must have been out with Louis, didn't we, Dora?"

"Oh, yes," she nodded enthusiastically. "Probably a date. Just the two of them."

The three men rubbed their chins and shifted in their seats.

"Say, it's lucky we ran into you two dames," Reilly said. "Sarge will want to hear that. We didn't realize about her dress."

"We'd better head back to the station," Peterson agreed. "Nice meeting you two."

The two of them moved to the door and began to pull on their standard-issue coats, scarves, and hats.

Officer Grey, however, lingered at the table. "I should probably get your address and telephone number, Miss Beaumont, in case we have any further questions."

Even I saw this for the ploy that it was. I doubted that Dora would be willing to give a lowly policeman the time of day, but she dug in her purse and pulled out one of her cards.

"I'll write my telephone number on the back." She winked and pulled a small pencil out. "Don't call too early in the morning. I need my beauty sleep."

Ted Grey took the card, nodded to us both, and went to join his friends at the door, who hooted when they saw Dora's card in his hand.

Once we were walking back home, I couldn't stand it any longer. "Why did you give Officer Grey your card?"

"Oh, Ruby," she sighed. "I'm never one to ignore a handsome young man. I guess I'm just too charitable for my own good."

It was our turn to hoot with laughter as we linked arms and headed home.

CHAPTER SEVEN

Aunt Muriel, I learned, was hosting her bridge group the second Saturday in December. This meant that we had to give the house a good cleaning and that I would be required to help serve her guests. Since the house was always spotless, I found the first request to be overkill. And, since I couldn't imagine anything worse than spending an afternoon being ordered around by Aunt Muriel and her friends, the second request made me groan internally and make aggravated faces behind my aunt's back.

For the next two days, we used and reused the same wash water while mopping all the floors. Windows were cleaned with a vinegar mixture Aunt Muriel swore by. The stove had to be blacked, though I'd never done the job before. Aunt Muriel began by instructing me how to do it until she grew frustrated that I wasn't doing *exactly* what she said *exactly* when she said to do it and snatched the rag out of my hand and did it herself. I was then treated to the sight of my aunt's bony behind sticking out as she scrubbed at the inside of the stove, her voice lecturing all the time.

We made a very thin punch and a sparse tray of cookies.

Before this, I'd imagined that I knew how to fill cups and carry a plate of cookies. My aunt, however, did not agree with that assessment of my hostess skills. As it turned out, there was an art to making a spinster's refreshments spread thinner than thin. I was not to fill cups above the halfway mark, which was the large leaf on the side of the rosebud on Aunt Muriel's heirloom glassware. I could replenish the cookies once, if Amanda Allen brought her sponge cake, and twice if she did not. Since there were eight ladies coming, the number of cookies on the plate should not exceed eight. And, it was perfectly acceptable to allow one cookie to linger since it would deter her guests from taking the last cookie, which would then require me to fill the tray lest we look like Cheap Charlies. I, of course, was not to have any refreshments until the end of the event and only if there were any left.

By the time the ladies began to arrive, I had a pounding headache. Aunt Muriel gave my new navy wool dress one more disapproving frown before squaring her round shoulders and opening the door. I hid a smile and smoothed the lacy apron I'd borrowed from Dora.

I'd expected Aunt Muriel's group of friends to be much like her. We'd interacted some at church, but I hadn't seen them outside the women's circle meetings, church services, and structured events. I learned that my assessment of them was wrong. A few ladies chattered away quite cheerfully. Several were pleasantly plump. Two even smiled warmly at me and engaged me in conversation. Of course, Aunt Muriel reigned over them all with an air of superiority which they seemed to tolerate pleasantly enough.

"It's so nice to meet you, Ruby, dear," Miss Olive Richardson smiled at me. "Muriel told us you'd be coming to live with her for a time."

"If you've survived this long, I think you've got a chance of making it for the long haul," Miss Irene Turner said with a twinkle in her eye. "I can say that without any malice because she, Olive, and I are the three spinsters of the group. We've known each other for more than three decades."

I liked these two. Miss Richardson was small and smiled softly while Miss Turner was big and broad and happy. They seemed like they were more than a match for Aunt Muriel. If they were also spinsters, it seemed hopeful that I wouldn't have to end up cross and crotchety after all. Maybe being an unmarried woman wasn't the worst thing that could happen to me.

Making my excuses, I moved on to visit with the other ladies. Mrs. Elmer Wick, Mrs. Claude Davenport, and Mrs. Guy Owens were discussing the weather and comparing it to past Decembers they remembered. We discussed the success of the last church supper and they thanked me for helping before moving on to the mysterious illness.

Their speculations only reminded me that it was one more puzzle I had yet to decipher and I was glad to find Mrs. Ida Mills lingering over the punch bowl by herself. I'd so enjoyed talking with her at the supper that I hoped she wouldn't go on and on about how worried she was about the food poisoning.

"How are you?" she asked amiably.

"I'm fine, thank you. Have you been staying warm?" I smiled at her.

"Of course, I have. I have a fur coat that I had made into long underwear. Didn't your aunt tell you?" She raised an eyebrow at me and sipped her punch.

I couldn't hide my grin, appreciating the joke at my aunt's expense. Without taking time to think about it, I pressed her, "Listen, Mrs. Mills, I wonder if I could ask you something about the deposit from the church supper."

Both eyebrows lifted at this. "What do you want to know?"

"Pastor Mason was called away suddenly when I was at the church and he asked me to take the money and deposit it. He said it was the proceeds from the supper, but it was more than two hundred dollars." My voice had dropped to a whisper. "You're the treasurer for the church. Is that sort of thing typical?"

"Your father is a minister, isn't he?" She waited for my nod. "Most people don't have any idea how a church is funded. They think food appears magically on the altar for the minister to eat."

I managed a tight smile.

Mrs. Mills sighed. "Someone made a very generous donation. The donor wished to remain anonymous and so I'm not surprised that Pastor Mason didn't mention anything to you." She looked around at the other ladies who were beginning to take their seats. "I appreciate you asking me about it privately. I doubt the donor would want word getting out about his generosity."

She patted my arm reassuringly and I felt better. Of course that was what had happened. The food poisoning must have set me seeing crime happening everywhere at church. It was such a relief to find a logical explanation.

Aunt Muriel came over and barked orders at me. The punch had gone quickly since Aunt Muriel hadn't made more than half a punchbowl full. She ordered me to brew a pot of tea, as though I had been the one to restrict the beverage allotment. Still, this command allowed me to escape to the kitchen while the ladies sat at the two card tables and began to shuffle, deal, and bid.

The afternoon crept by. It became apparent that Aunt Muriel was smugly good at bridge. Her only real competition was Mrs. Mills, whose imperious tone as she made her bids rivaled my aunt's. Mrs. Mills was every bit as clever and strategic as my aunt. I could feel the palpable tension their personal competition created. When Aunt Muriel lost, her sour face ushered everyone out the door with all the haste they could manage while not giving outright offense.

In fact, the ladies left so quickly that one of them left a tapestry bag behind. I found it tucked between two chair legs while I was putting the card tables away. I peeked inside, hoping to find a clue as to the owner without having to dig too deeply. There was a crumpled handkerchief, a small figurine with pointy ears, and a ledger.

There was no hope for it. I would have to open the ledger to find out to whom the bag belonged. Feeling like I was betraying someone's confidence, I slid the book out and opened it. Inside the front cover were the words "Port Vernon Methodist Church." I cocked my head. This was an account book for the church. Therefore, the bag could only belong to Ida Mills.

With that mystery solved, I should have tucked the ledger back into the bag and let Aunt Muriel know. Something made me flip through the pages, though. I admired the tidy handwriting and meticulous accounting while remembering Mrs. Mills' quips about my aunt. The more I learned about the lady, the more I liked her.

I stopped at the last page and my eyes scanned the column of numbers. My heart started beating faster before my brain registered what was wrong. I ran a finger down the column and then under the entry for the word "deposit." There it was, in black and white. The date for the church supper had an entry for eleven dollars and thirty cents.

Below it was the amount for the deposit. I double checked the date and saw that it was, indeed, the deposit I'd taken to the bank. The total was for twenty-three dollars and eighty-four cents.

I could feel my mind whirling. Why wouldn't Mrs. Mills write down the correct deposit amount? Surely she would have to list any donations in the record book. An anonymous donor couldn't object to that. I sat back, more confused than ever. I wanted to believe Mrs. Mills' explanation, but it just didn't add up.

"She's as rich as Midas," Aunt Muriel informed me as we washed up later that evening. "Her late husband was in shipping and he made a bundle. Ida's on good terms with Geraldine Beaumont," Aunt Muriel continued. The sniff of contempt that accompanied this told me exactly what my aunt thought of the Beaumonts.

"Why don't you like them?" I pressed, momentarily distracted from the problem of Mrs. Mills.

"It's not Christian to dislike people," she scolded automatically.

I raised an eyebrow at her as she passed me a plate to dry and a slightly guilty expression paused on her face for the briefest of moments. Then Aunt Muriel straightened her shoulders, chewed her lips for a moment, and went on in an imperious tone.

"You might as well know that Clarence Beaumont is a philanderer and everyone knows it."

My dish towel stopped moving. Dora's father was unfaithful to her mother? How awful. It momentarily pushed the ledger out of my mind.

"Is that why you dislike them?" I had to ask.

Aunt Muriel appeared to be deciding whether or not to hold her tongue or spill what she knew. Finally, the dam broke and she said, "The wealthy families in this town think that they are above the law. They flout Prohibition and have no qualms about less-than-honest business dealings. It's why I don't like you going around with the Beaumont girl all the time."

Ah, so that was it. Aunt Muriel was, as I'd suspected, overly fond of following rules. At least, she was fond of the rules she wanted to follow. Well, Dora was my only friend in Port Vernon and I wasn't about to let her go because her parents weren't as law-abiding as my aunt would have liked.

"I promise to be careful, Aunt Muriel, but I won't stop spending time over there. Dora is paying me to be her secretary. Also, Charlie said I was a good influence on her and I agree."

I could tell Aunt Muriel didn't like that answer, but she wasn't about to argue about me earning money. It looked like Dora's plan was working.

By the time I finished my chores to Aunt Muriel's meticulous standards the next day and escaped through the fence to the Beaumont's house, Ted Grey had already called Dora.

"He asked if I would be interested in 'further discussing the case' at the pictures tonight," Dora laughed. "I would have refused him, but it was such a good try that I just couldn't bring myself to do it."

"That was fast work," I said as I removed my coat and hat.

"Say, why don't you and Charlie come along? We'll call it a double date and then if it turns out he's a milquetoast, it'll be easier for me to give him the bum's rush." She leaned over her dressing table to examine her makeup. "Besides, I don't want to go to the petting pantry with just anyone. He might get the wrong idea."

"Petting pantry?"

"You know, the theater." She caught my eye in the mirror and one thin, penciled eyebrow lifted. "You've been petting before, haven't you, Ruby?"

Blushing a little, I shook my head. "I've never been on a date before."

She turned around on the bench, looking at me in shock. "You've *never* gone on a date before?"

Shrugging uncomfortably, I explained, "My father was the minister in a country church. There weren't many boys around and they were too scared to ask the minister's daughter out. Besides, there wasn't much to do for fun that wasn't a church-sponsored event. It wouldn't be much of a date with my parents and the rest of the congregation acting as chaperones."

Dora came and stood before me. She took both my hands in hers and looked up at me with large, watery eyes. "I always knew that it was my duty to introduce you to the world. But not until this very moment did I realize just how devastatingly dull your life has been. Don't worry, Ruby, you can trust your old Auntie Dora. I'll introduce you to all the good things in life."

A smile struggled onto my lips and I said, "Gee, thanks."

Just then, Minnie burst through the door.

"Get out!" Dora was instantly outraged at her younger sister.

Minnie stuck out her tongue. "Do you want me to get out or do you want to know that there's someone at the door for you?"

Dora shoved her sister out of the way and charged down

the stairs. I paused to make sure that Minnie was steady on her feet and gave her an apologetic smile before following Dora to the kitchen door.

My heart gave a funny jolt when I saw Gus standing there. He looked up from Dora, a frown on his lips, and shot me a friendly grin.

"What are you doing here?" Dora demanded.

"I think I've found someone you two dames need to talk to," Gus answered easily.

"Who?" I asked a little too quickly.

"Jean Waldeck's brother, Gordon."

"Gordon Waldeck?" scoffed Dora. "He's in the loony bin."

Gus frowned at her. "No, he's in a sanatorium. The state sanatorium, that is."

"It's the same thing," Dora waved a hand to brush off his words.

"Hardly." Gus glared at my friend.

"Where is that?" I motioned for Gus to come in and the three of us settled at the kitchen table.

"It's outside Detroit, not 30 miles from here." He leaned forward. "Now, I know they don't usually let strangers in to see the patients, but I happen to know one of the orderlies there. He'll find a way for at least one of us to get in and ask Gord some questions. We won't have long, but it's possible that we could learn something interesting."

I was ready to go. "How do we get there?"

"That's the part I'm stuck on," Gus admitted.

We both turned to Dora, who looked between us doubtfully. "You want us to drive all the way to the state sanatorium in order to ask crazy Gord Waldeck about his sister? He doesn't know what month it is. Why do you think he'd know anything about Jean?"

It was a fair question and I looked back at Gus for an answer.

He seemed to be considering whether or not to divulge more information to us. After a long moment, he nodded slightly and then said, "I've been hearing things about Louis Hardy and some illegal activities he's gotten involved with recently."

"We already know he's a smuggler," Dora said, her voice accusatory. "Gin and dope, right? That's what that Liam fellow told us."

"Well, some are saying that Hardy is doing more than just smuggling it."

"What do you mean?" My forehead creased and I again despaired at how naïve I was about crime.

"Some people are saying that he's helping to distribute it." Gus waited for us to understand. When our faces remained blank he sighed and went on, "Either Hardy's got a network of people selling drugs for him, or he's working for a bigwig who's running a network and Hardy's high up the ladder."

I chewed my thumbnail absently. Smuggling was dangerous work. Still, someone who could sell drugs to people was a different kind of criminal entirely. It would be someone who was so greedy that he didn't care about the toll that those drugs would take on any users.

"Let's think about this for a minute." I began to brainstorm out loud. "Jean's brother has had trouble with drugs of some sort or another. She was sensitive enough about it to be really upset when you brought it up at the party, Dora. There's no way that she would have been involved with a drug dealer. It would have been one thing if she'd found out he was bringing drugs over the border and another if she knew he was involved in selling them. She might have been willing to break it off with Hardy."

"There's no way she would have sat back and let him sell them to locals," Gus agreed. "If she had found out about that, she would have gone straight to the police."

"And Hardy wouldn't have allowed that." I nodded. It all made sense.

"I don't know," interjected Dora. "It sounds like it could happen, but we don't have any proof that it did. All Gus has said is that he's heard rumors that Hardy is selling drugs. Liam heard rumors that the *Baker's Dozen* is bringing them in from Canada. It's all just hearsay. We can't go to the police with that."

I nodded at her, impressed. Then, turning back to Gus, I said, "I think we need to go see Gord Waldeck."

Dora sighed noisily. "I'll go and see if Charlie can drive us."

As it turned out, Charlie was more than willing. He worked intermittently at his father's office downtown. I didn't understand why he was allowed to spend so much time out of the office, but whatever arrangement they had seemed to work for the Beaumont men.

We spent the first part of the drive getting Charlie up to speed on what we knew about Jean's death. Charlie whistled when he heard what we were planning to do.

"You're getting involved with some dangerous people," he worried, catching my eye in the mirror. "If I'd known that this was what you had in mind, I never would have agreed to it. It's possible that Louis Hardy is paying someone to keep an eye on Gordon Waldeck."

"Why would he do that?" Dora asked sharply.

Charlie shrugged. "He's not the only one at the sanatorium who's there for being addicted to drugs. If I was Hardy, I'd want to know if the people who are there are talking to the police. They'd be easy targets in a hospital if they checked in with drug-related problems."

I hadn't thought about that. "What should we do? I really think we need to talk to Gord, but I don't want to put us in any danger."

"We can tell them that we're friends of Jean's and that we want to console her brother after her death," Dora suggested.

Finally, I took charge. "Dora, why don't you work your magic on the patients and nurses? Perhaps if Hardy's spies think you're here for some other reason, they won't notice how long we're talking with Gord."

I looked to Charlie to see what he thought. He exchanged a look with Gus, who nodded slowly.

"That could work. You won't have much time, though. If you're just visiting to talk about Jean, you wouldn't need more than a few minutes."

We arrived at the sanatorium in good time. We had to go through a gate, past a guard, and wind up the long drive to the front doors. As we climbed out of the car, I looked up and felt generally disappointed at the neat, white, rectangular building in front of us. Even the bright sky failed to contribute to the atmosphere. Shouldn't the whole place have more of an aura of menace? I'd expected some crumbling, sinister manor with barred windows and creepy dying trees baring their branches at us threateningly.

Gus led us into the main building and we found ourselves in a clean, modern reception area with doors opening into a large, bright room where the patients were occupied in a variety of activities. Nurses in crisp uniforms bustled about their business. Orderlies milled around, helping patients in wheelchairs or sitting at tables. A young nurse hurried over to us, clipboard in hand.

"Good afternoon," she chirped. "How many I help you?"

"Oh, we're here to see John Wallace," Gus dismissed her as an orderly made a beeline for Gus.

The two men nodded a greeting to each other. Apparently this was John Wallace who was to be our connection to Gord Waldeck. I looked him over speculatively. If orderlies needed to be tall and strong, then John Wallace was the man for the job. Surely even someone who wasn't in his right mind would think twice before taking on this fellow.

"Thank you, nurse," Wallace said. "These are friends of mine."

He led us away, the nurse looking skeptical behind us for a moment until a patient's outburst of laughter drew her attention. We were ushered into a small waiting room.

"I'll bring Gord here," the big man explained. "However, he might not talk to so many of you."

Dora shot him her most winning smile. "Golly, Mr. Wallace, I am *so* interested in becoming a nurse. Do you think anyone would mind if I asked a few questions of the nurses and patients?"

Charlie's loud laugh earned him a gouge in the ribs from his sister's elbow. "I'll go with you, sis," he amended hastily.

"I'll be right back," Wallace agreed.

Less than a minute later, he backed into the room, pulling a wheelchair. After one look at the man in the chair, Dora's face constricted and she hurried out of the room. Charlie gave us a bracing look before following his sister.

Gus pulled up chairs facing the man huddled pitifully

in the wheelchair and I sat down. Then I turned my attention to Gord Waldeck. It took all of my presence of mind to keep my face neutral.

The man sitting across from us was withered. He was thin and twitched occasionally. If I hadn't known better, I would have guessed that he was Jean's father instead of her brother. Gord scratched at a red, raw patch on his left arm and struggled to meet our eyes. The worst part of all, though, was that his nose had been partly eaten away, by years of sniffing cocaine, I guessed.

I pressed my lips together, too shocked to find words. I'd never in my life been face to face with a man whose vices had robbed him of so much. Pity and sympathy warred with anger and condemnation. What had to happen in a person's life to make him give up everything for the fleeting respite of drug use?

Thankfully, Gus recovered from his shock before I did. "Gord, my name is Gus and this is Ruby. We want to talk to you about your sister Jean."

Gord shook his head slowly and in a hollow voice said, "Jean's dead."

"We know. We were hoping to ask some questions about her." Gus shot me a look that expressed his doubt in Gord's ability to cooperate.

"She's dead," he repeated, scratching at his arm without noticing.

I had to step in. "We're helping the police to find out who killed her. Do you think you could help us?"

Gord wrestled his eyes to mine. After a long moment, he nodded.

My heart lifted. "Jean was dating Louis Hardy before she died. We believe that he's involved in smuggling and selling drugs. Do you know anything about that?"

His eyes roamed to the window before he nodded again.

"Is Louis directly in charge of selling drugs or does he work for someone?" I didn't know whether or not the question was relevant, but I had to keep Gord involved until I could think of something better to ask.

"He works for someone."

"Who?" Gus asked quickly.

Gord shrugged one thin shoulder. "Some swell in town. No one knows who."

"Is there a local gangster?" I looked at Gus for the answer, but it was Gord who replied.

"No. It's some rich sheik. Only Hardy knows who it is."

I sat back in my chair. Someone in town was bringing over drugs from Canada and selling them to locals. Louis Hardy worked for this person and was the only one who knew his identity. What if Jean had found out who it was? Louis Hardy wouldn't have been the only one who wanted her dead.

"How do you know about this?" Gus asked.

Gord smiled mirthlessly. "I helped Louis on the boat and I sold for him among the society swells."

"But you didn't know who you were really working for," I pressed.

"If I knew that, I would be dead."

At that moment, the door was flung open and a group of nurses burst in.

"What is going on in here?" the oldest one demanded. "This man is very sick and isn't allowed visitors who aren't family members."

I looked up at the women and tried to guess whether or not they were working for Louis Hardy. What did they see here? What could they report back?

With much stammering and inventing, Gus tried to

sooth the angry group who immediately fussed over Gord before wheeling him away while throwing reproving looks at us. When his protestations and blatant lies failed to work, we were unceremoniously escorted out of the building and told not to return. Only a few moments later, Charlie and Dora were deposited on the sidewalk next to us.

"Let's get out of here," Gus said. He and Charlie shared a serious nod and the four of us walked as fast as we could to the car.

It wasn't until we were a few miles down the road that we breathed a collective sigh of relief.

"That could have gone much worse," Dora crowed. "I really had them going with my 'my dearest ambition is to follow in your footsteps' spiel."

Charlie gave his sister a wide smile. "I have to hand it to you, sis. That was some performance you put on. Lillian Gish couldn't have done it better herself when she was on the stage in New York City, thrilling audiences."

"Thank you, dear brother," Dora said in a lofty voice.

"Did you two learn anything from Gord?" Charlie steered the conversation to us and

we filled the pair of them in on what Gord had said.

"Good," Dora said once we'd finished. "Now we can turn that over to the police and be done with this whole thing. I don't want to be involved anymore."

I saw Gus and Charlie exchange knowing looks. "It's not that easy, Dora," I explained gently. "We still don't have any real evidence."

"We don't need evidence," she argued. "That's for the police to discover. All we have to do is give them suggestions of what is likely and they can do the dangerous work themselves. Tonight you and Charlie and I will tell Ted about Louis and the drugs. We don't have to say that we talked to

Gord Waldeck. We can just suggest that we heard that there's someone in town running a big drug operation."

It was a good point. Since none of the rest of us were too keen on sticking our noses into really dangerous spots, we talked it over and agreed that Dora's plan was the best one we had.

CHAPTER EIGHT

Thanks to Dora, we both were dressed, coiffed, and made up perfectly for our double date. Dora decided that I'd already worn the new dress she'd bought me too many times around Charlie. She flicked through her closet and chose a berry-colored dress for me and midnight blue one for herself. Even though we had completely different builds, Dora's dress fit me fairly well. She chose coordinating coats and cloches and we were ready to go.

"Does this Ted chap know we're doubling?" Charlie asked his sister as we pulled out of the driveway in his always-shining gray car.

"Nope," Dora sang, struggling to put on lipstick as we lurched down the dirt alley to the main road.

"That's a low blow to a fellow's pride, Dora," her brother chastised.

I sat in the back seat and had to agree with Charlie. We were going to be a very unwelcome surprise. However, this didn't seem to bother Dora one bit. She looked over her shoulder at me and gave me an impish grin.

Sure enough, when we arrived at the theater, Ted Grey

was waiting anxiously while trying not to look it. I thought it was sweet. Dora, on the other hand, rolled her eyes and sighed in a long-suffering way.

"Hey there," Ted called as soon as we drew close. His eyes had been fixed on Dora since he'd spotted her and it took him a while to register that she wasn't alone. When Ted finally looked over and saw me and Charlie, his eager grin slipped slightly.

"Ted, you remember Ruby." Dora made smug introductions. "This is my brother Charlie. I thought it would be fun to turn this date into a double."

Well, there was really nothing that Ted could say to that. He forced a grin back on his face and led the way to the ticket booth, Dora preening beside him. Charlie and I shook our heads at each other and followed the others.

The picture was *Beau Brummel*, starring John Barrymore. Dora had seen it before, but it was new to me. I was quickly caught up in the organ music and red velvet curtains and beautiful costumes. In fact, I was so enraptured that I almost didn't notice when Charlie slid his arm behind me and dropped it onto my shoulder.

I looked down at his hand and back up at my date. Charlie winked at me and turned his attention back to the screen. I wasn't sure what to make of this and looked over to Dora. She was watching the picture with a rather grumpy look on her face. Ted, I noticed, was sitting as stiff as a poker on her other side, his hands carefully resting on his knees. I wondered if Dora was upset that he wasn't trying to put the moves on her despite everything she'd said to the contrary.

When nothing further happened either with Dora's date's hands or Charlie's, I focused back on the moving picture in front of us and was soon caught up in the story again. By the time the lights came up, Dora was sniffling in her handkerchief. I'd found the ending silly and hadn't been remotely tempted to tear up. However, I patted my friend on the back until she was able to get herself under control.

Ted looked at the three of us, self-doubt written all over his face. I was mildly irritated with Dora for treating a nice young man so badly. He had taken a risk and asked her out and she'd been a real heel. With a quick glance at Charlie, I made up my mind.

"Why don't we go somewhere for a soda?" I suggested.

The fellows both were in favor of this idea and we all moved to the aisle as the two of them made plans. Dora pulled me back and frowned at me.

"Why did you say that?" she hissed.

"You're being really unfair to Ted," I scolded. "He's very excited to be on a date with you and you pulled a mean trick bringing us along without telling him. The least you can do is get a soda with him and be polite."

Dora pouted. "I told you he was a milquetoast. He didn't so much as try and hold my hand during the movie. Even Charlie put an arm around you."

My scolding must have affected her though, because by the time we slid into the booth at the drugstore she had clearly decided to win Ted over and was pulling out all the stops. I could tell from his delighted responses to her laughter and attention that this was what he'd hoped his date with Dora would be like.

"How's the soda?" Charlie asked quietly in my ear as he slid his arm across the back of the booth. It meant that I was pressed up against his side, but I found that it wasn't an unpleasant place to be.

"It's very good." I smiled up at him.

Charlie grinned back and then we started the plan we'd discussed on the drive to the movie theater.

"Say, Ted, you're a cop, right?" Charlie asked.

Ted dragged his eyes from Dora's pretty, animated face and nodded at her brother.

"I imagine that you fellows have your hands full with all the smuggling up and down the border."

"Sure," Ted nodded. "The Coast Guard helps, but we have a lot of work trying to track down what comes over from Canada. When it's cold enough and the river freezes, some smugglers drive their cars back and forth over the ice."

"Isn't that dangerous?" Dora gasped.

Her date shrugged. "For people who are willing to break the law, I suppose they think the risk is worth it."

"Do they just smuggle gin?" I asked innocently.

"No way." Ted was warming up to the topic now. "Quite a lot of drugs are being brought over, too."

"Drugs?" I put as much surprise into the word as I could. "Where do the drugs go? Chicago? New York?"

"Unfortunately, they get pedaled around Port Vernon."

"Really?" Dora was not entirely convincing and I pressed my foot over hers under the table. She frowned at me in response.

Charlie stepped in quickly. "I've heard rumors that there's a society swell who runs the whole thing here in town."

We all watched Ted carefully for his reaction.

He took a long drink of his soda and then nonchalantly nodded. "That's true. We don't know who it is, but we do know it's someone in business in town. Maybe a lawyer or doctor even. He's wealthy enough to own a ritzy boat that's fast and quiet and doesn't care about what drugs do to the people who take them."

The three of us deflated slightly. None of this was news

to us and our information had obviously not added to Ted's knowledge either.

"Just think," Ted continued, "he's probably a family man with a wife and kids and everything. He leads an entire life that his family knows nothing about. I bet he has all sorts of girlfriends on the side like a real gangster. Oh, and a boat, of course," He shook his head. "I wouldn't want to be his son when we catch him. He'll head off to jail and his family will be humiliated."

Charlie and Dora exchanged a worried look. I bit my lip. A family man who was in business, was unfaithful to his wife, and had a boat. With a description like that, it sounded like Mr. Beaumont could be the leader of the ring. Was this why he was anxious to sell his boat? Was he afraid it would link him to the crime? What if the *Baker's Dozen* was only one of the boats used for smuggling? But that was ridiculous, I chided myself. Wasn't it?

Apparently Charlie and Dora didn't think so. The mood shifted subtly after that. Charlie grew quiet and Dora became even more animated. I sat watching the pair of them process the idea that their own father might be the head of a drug ring, not knowing what to do or say to help.

"I want to go for a walk," Dora announced. "Ted, what do you say?"

"Dora ..." I put out a hand to her, but she brushed me off.

"Ruby, I'll be with a police officer, for crying out loud. What could be safer?" Then she was swinging out of the booth and sashaying out the door. I watched Ted watch her go, a little dazed, before he gathered his wits and followed her outside.

I blew out my breath and turned my attention on Charlie. My date was sitting, fiddling with a paper straw from the dispenser on the table. A dark cloud had settled firmly over him.

"It isn't your father, Charlie," I blurted without preamble.

He turned bleak eyes to me. "How do you know that? You can't know for certain."

It was a fair point. I didn't really know that Mr. Beaumont was innocent. I hardly knew the man.

"I hate him," Charlie growled.

I looked at him in surprise. "Why do you say that?"

Charlie looked down at his hands and softly said, "He has a girlfriend." I gasped, but Charlie kept talking, as though he needed to get it all out. "He's had a few of them over the years. I learned about it when I was a kid. He's got an apartment downtown where he keeps her."

I put my hand on his and he grabbed onto it as though he was a drowning man and I was a life preserver.

"He works all the time. At least, he tells Mother he works all the time. He's out of the office plenty, though. I know he goes to parties with his friends or gets drunk at his club. It's as though he'd rather be anywhere than at home with his family."

"Do you want to know what I think?" I asked quietly.

He nodded quickly.

"I think you love your father and you've been waiting your whole life for him to show that he loves you back. He's been so busy with everything else that he's ignored you and your family."

Charlie squeezed my hand, looking, for once, like a little boy instead of a confident young man who knew too much about the world.

"Imagine what your father must be feeling," I went on.

"Something must be driving him to get drunk and chase girls."

"I don't have to imagine. I know what makes him feel that way," Charlie admitted sadly. "It's the same thing that makes me go to parties and fool around with girls I don't even like." He chewed his lip as the silence stretched. "Do you think my grandfather ignored his family, too?"

"It's possible," I shrugged. It wasn't really my business, but I couldn't stop myself from going on. "Charlie, if you don't want to follow in their footsteps, then you have to be the one to make the changes in your life. You don't have to go to parties and get drunk or do drugs."

His eyes swung to mine, clearly surprised and embarrassed.

"Dora told me." I waved his concern away. "You get to choose to be your own man. Why not change things now so that, when the time comes, you can be the father you wish you had? Your children won't have to feel the way you and Dora do."

I could tell that Charlie was getting emotional and he didn't want to show it, especially not here in the middle of the drugstore. "Why don't we call it a night?" I suggested gently.

We rode home in silence. I thought that was the end of things but Charlie insisted on walking me to my door. We stood awkwardly on the stoop, not sure how to bring the strange night to a close.

"This isn't how I wanted our first date to go," Charlie finally said.

I cocked my head. "It isn't?" He'd thought about going on a date with me before? I'd assumed that he'd only agreed because his sister had insisted.

He laughed softly. "I hadn't planned on bringing Dora along or doing detective work."

It was my turn to chuckle.

"I just couldn't get my courage up to ask you." Charlie's eyes were serious.

There was something surreal about standing on my aunt's front stoop with Charlie Beaumont admitting that he had been too scared to ask me on a date. He was the sort of boy that confidently asked out any girl he wanted. He'd been on dozens of dates, surely.

"I want to ask to kiss you goodnight," he said almost shyly. "But I'm going to wait until we go on a real first date. Can I get a rain heck?"

I opened my mouth to try and say something, though I wasn't sure what. To my great relief, footsteps in the alley drew our attention away from the intensity of the moment.

"Who's there?" Charlie called.

A figure lurched out of the darkness. At first, I couldn't tell who it was, but a few steps later, Gus' battered face came into sharper focus.

"Gus?" I cried.

Charlie and I both hurried over and helped him into the house. The next minutes were filled with my clumsy attempts at first aid while Charlie telephoned for a doctor. Gus didn't say much while I mopped him up. By the time Charlie was back, I had the dried blood off Gus' face and could see that he had a nasty cut near his hairline, a split lip, and a blackened eye. From the way he was clutching his midsection, I guessed he had at least a bruised rib to add to the list of injuries.

Aunt Muriel arrived downstairs around the same time that the doctor did and I had my hands full with filling her in.

"Ruby Jean, that young man cannot stay here," she barked once she realized that Gus' injuries were too serious to send him home. "What would the neighbors think if they saw him coming out of our house in the morning? They'd assume this is some sort of den of iniquity." She clutched the chest of her dressing gown as though to keep prying eyes away.

"We're going to do whatever the doctor says," I said staunchly. "And since the Beaumonts are our neighbors, I'm sure Charlie will fill them in on what happened. Why don't you put the kettle on? The doctor will probably welcome a cup of tea on this cold night."

I left her spluttering indignantly in the kitchen, though she was reaching for the knob on the stove when I peeked over my shoulder. The doctor had finished stitching Gus' head and was wrapping it with a white bandage.

"What happened?" I asked Charlie quietly.

"He says he got in a fight, but I don't think he wants to say anything in front of the doctor," Charlie said in a low voice. "Since he came here, I'm guessing this has something to do with Jean's death."

I bit my lip. How could it be related to Jean's death? Had Gus been attacked because I'd asked him to get involved? If that was true, I didn't know how I would forgive myself. It had all seemed so innocent when we'd started asking questions. Gus' battered face was making the dangers much more real than anything had before. Jean had been murdered by someone who wanted to keep her quiet and now we were unearthing the very secrets that had gotten her killed. Had I brought trouble on my friends? Was Aunt Muriel in danger because of my curiosity? Terrible guilt swallowed me as I watched Gus wince away from the doctor's touch.

CHAPTER NINE

The doctor gave Gus something to help with the pain that put him to sleep pretty quickly. I made sure he had plenty of blankets and then went back to the kitchen with the others.

"He'll sleep all night," the doctor explained, accepting a steaming china cup from Aunt Muriel. "He should be ready to go home tomorrow, though. You won't have to keep him here long."

Aunt Muriel reluctantly acquiesced, though she did insist on seeing both Charlie and the doctor out before escorting me upstairs and waiting while I turned the lock on my bedroom door.

As I tossed and turned, I mulled over my motivations for the case and asked God if I was right to keep investigating Jean's murder. Why was it that the most painful decisions were always the ones where two good things battled each other? Finding justice for Jean was a good thing, but so was protecting my friends. Was it worth risking our lives to find out the truth? Before, when it was just a matter of Jean's death, I might have said no. Now that we were looking at finding the leader of a drug ring who was harming hundreds, maybe even thousands, of people, I wasn't so sure.

Despite my late night, I was up early, anxious to check on our patient. Gus was still snoring when I leaned nervously over him, so I made my way to the kitchen and began to cook breakfast. Aunt Muriel was sure to scold me for it, but I needed to do something with my hands and I began mixing up a big batch of pancake batter and pulled out a rasher of bacon to go with it.

Things were progressing well when the padding of feet behind me announced Gus' presence. I turned and grimaced at the sight of him. His eye was black and blue, his lip still swollen, and the white bandage encircling his head made him look like a wounded soldier.

"What am I doing here, Ruby?" he asked groggily.

"How are you feeling today?"

"Like I was on the losing end of five rounds with Jack Dempsey. You didn't happen to find me on the floor of a boxing ring, did you?"

I smiled shakily, glad that he still had his sense of humor. "Do you remember anything from last night?"

Gus sat heavily in one of the kitchen chairs and dropped his head in his hand. "Ouch," he moaned, head snapping back up. "Oh, now I remember."

I began to set the table and bring over the food. "Coffee?"

"Sure." He stretched and then reached for his ribs with another groan.

Once everything was on the table, I sat down. "Are you hungry today?"

"Starving." Gus grinned a little lopsidedly before reaching for the pancakes. He held the plate up for me to help myself before choosing pancakes for himself. The gesture warmed me in a way that Charlie's arm around my shoulders hadn't.

We busied ourselves with coffee and syrup and bacon for a few minutes. Once we were both chewing, I felt free to ask all the questions that had been burning in my mind since he'd appeared out of the dark last night.

"What happened to you? And why did you come here?" I asked around a syrupy bit. In my curiosity, I seemed to forget all the manners my mother had taught me.

Gus chewed slowly for a moment before taking a swig of coffee. He glanced up at me and cocked an eyebrow. "Hardy's men jumped me last night. There were at least three of them."

I clutched at my chest in a move that was reminiscent of my aunt. "Hardy's men? Why would they attack you, Gus?"

"They told me to keep my nose out of their boss' business or else they'd come after you." His dark eyes were intense. "Someone from the sanatorium must have told him we talked with Gord. I fought them off and knew I had to come and warn you. Ruby, you've got to stop looking into this thing."

I toyed with my fork. "Last night I was thinking the same thing, but I came to the conclusion that we can't stop." I smiled apologetically at him.

Gus was agitated. "That's crazy talk. Jean Waldeck was killed for this. Are you willing to lose your life too?"

"In order to stop a drug lord from hurting people? Yes, I am." I was growing passionate about the topic. "You saw Gord yesterday. You were just as horrified by his state as I was. That's what drugs do to people. If we can find out who is behind the smuggling and stop him, then maybe we can save someone else from that fate."

Gus appraised me. "You're willing to risk your life for people you don't even know?" His tone was three parts scorn and one part admiration.

My face was too hot from arguing to grow warmer but I felt that admiration deep down in my belly. I looked down and shrugged. "If someone came after you, then we're on the right track. Maybe we're close to figuring out who it is that's funding Louis Hardy's smuggling. And as soon as we do that, we'll head right to the police."

He looked at me as though he'd never seen anyone like me before. Finally, Gus looked away and shook his head in defeat. "All right, but we need to stay together. No going off on your own at night or walking around town with just Dora. Charlie or I should be with you at all times."

I nodded and we ate in silence for a full minute until Aunt Muriel arrived.

"Well, I see you're better and eating us out of house and home," she snipped.

I sighed and shot Gus an apologetic grimace. He, on the other hand, smiled charmingly.

"Gee, I sure appreciate your hospitality, Miss Barnes. I'm sorry to have been so much trouble. I'll be out your hair just as soon as I can be."

To my surprise, Aunt Muriel took the bait like a hungry fish and her frosty expression melted a little. She waved off his words and settled primly in a chair at the end of the table. Gus deftly moved all the dishes within her reach and even got up to get her a fresh cup of coffee. By the time her plate was full, my aunt was officially charmed.

Gus entertained us both with funny stories about when he worked at a pickle factory. His descriptions of the customers, owner, and other employees were both humorous and clever. At times, he stopped just this side of something crass and would wink cheekily at Aunt Muriel who tittered in response, knowing full well what he had barely avoided saying. Then he would shoot me a look that told me that he knew exactly how well he was winning over my aunt.

Once the plates were empty, she actually refused his help to clean up and insisted that he rest on the sofa before he head home. I was not excused, however, and was ordered to wash up the mess I'd made with an extra caution to not be wasteful with the soap. I shook my head as I scrubbed, both annoyed at Aunt Muriel and tickled by Gus' charming ways.

Maybe that was the problem, I mused as I took the wash water to dump in the backyard. Even though I knew that Gus was very handsome, perhaps I was only drawn to him because he was charming. He knew how to make women do what he wanted. I scowled at that thought. Was he just manipulating me? Was that all this was? All the times I'd thought that he might be a little bit extra fond of me, had I simply been falling under his spell? I didn't like that thought much at all.

In fact, I was so bent out of shape and wrapped up in my thoughts that I didn't hear the man who came from behind the back shed until he was right behind me. There was no time for me to do anything but let out a tiny cry of surprise as one of his arms snaked around me, pinning my arms down, and the other arm came up to clamp a hand tightly over my nose and mouth.

No matter how hard I struggled, I couldn't shake him loose. Even stomping on his foot only caused the brute to squeeze me harder. I couldn't breathe and my lungs began to constrict. His hand pinched my nose and firmly sealed my mouth closed. My brain began to panic as it became oxygen deprived.

"Keep your nose out of the Waldeck affair," his gravelly voice grated in my ear, "or next time you won't wake up."

Spots began to blot out the edges of my vision as I grew limp and everything went dark.

I swam back to wakefulness as though through a muddy swamp. It took me several blinking seconds before I realized that the fuzzy shape above me was a face and a few more seconds before I knew that the face looking down on me belonged to Charlie Beaumont.

"She's awake," he called over his shoulder before scooping me into his arms and jostling me in the direction of the house.

The journey made me dizzy and I squeezed my eyes shut, though I was aware of Dora's tearful voice weaving into Gus' worried one, punctuated by Aunt Muriel's sharp commands. Finally, I was deposited on the sofa, the world stopped jiggling, and I was able to open my eyes again.

"What happened?" I asked as each of them found seats nearby, watching me intently.

Dora threw herself onto the sofa beside me and took my hand. Speaking as though I was on death's doorstep, she said, "Gus found you in the back yard. You'd fainted or something."

"Should we call the doctor?" Charlie perched on the edge of a chair and leaned forward, ready for action.

The memory of my struggle with the stranger came back to me and I glanced quickly at my aunt before shaking my head. I didn't want her to know what had happened. If she thought I'd just had a silly fainting episode, she would be less afraid.

Gus, however, was suspicious. "Did someone do this to you?"

I tried to clue him into my reluctance to say something in front of Aunt Muriel, but he either didn't pick up on my pointed look or he wasn't going to play along.

"Was it one of Hardy's men?" he pressed.

"What are you talking about?" Aunt Muriel interjected, her voice splitting open our secret with the force of an ice pick.

I considered bluffing it out but I hadn't been raised to be dishonest and I knew that lying would only complicate matters unnecessarily. So I took a deep breath and gave her a simplified version of what we'd been up to, touching only briefly on the more dangerous aspects and completely leaving out the fact that Gus had been hurt by these men. There was no way, though, to avoid the fact that I'd been attacked by one of Hardy's emissaries.

"We need to call the police," Charlie insisted at the end of my recitation. Without waiting for a discussion as to the wisdom of this, Charlie went to the telephone and put the call through.

We sat around in awkward silence, listening as he made the report. Finally, Gus asked me how I was feeling.

I looked over at him and read such sincere concern in his eyes that I forgot my earlier anger about his charming ways and gave him a quavering smile.

"I think I'm all right. My head hurts, but my vision is clear and I remember what happened. No permanent damage." I tried to sound glib.

"You've all been very foolish." Aunt Muriel finally began the lecture that I'd known was building inside her. "Murders are for the police to work out, not young people. You are putting yourselves in grave danger. If I'd had any idea that you were involved in such things, I would have put a stop to it long ago."

The seed of rebellion that usually lived dormant in my mind began to unfurl as had become all too familiar when my aunt lectured me. Doing what was right was worth the cost and I had no intention of stopping.

Something must have registered on my face because Gus got to his feet and asked Aunt Muriel if she'd like him to check that the locks on the windows and doors were all in good working order. She was momentarily taken aback by this offer but quickly recovered and agreed. The two headed off upstairs and we could hear their footsteps echoing from above as they moved from room to room.

"I hope they don't send Ted," Dora said once my aunt was out of earshot.

Suddenly, I remembered that I hadn't had time to ask about how the rest of Dora's date had gone. I now guessed that it hadn't ended well.

"What happened on your walk?"

She became instantly squirrelly and refused to meet my eyes. "Nothing much," Dora said as she jiggled her leg and fiddled with her necklace.

I eyed her suspiciously. "Really nothing?"

She let out a dramatic sigh and rolled her eyes. "All right, it wasn't exactly nothing." She checked to see that her brother was still busy on the telephone before quietly divulging the details. "Ted was perfectly nice. He kept trying to talk, but I was distracted. You know, about Daddy ..." Her face became so dark that I reached over and took her hand. She managed a sad smile and went on. "So, to shut him up, we stopped in a dark spot and petted for a while."

"What?" I hissed. "You petted with Ted? Dora, it was your first date with him!"

My friend snatched her hand back and said defensively, "Well, I had just learned that my father might be in charge of a drug ring. You can't blame a girl for wanting to get her mind off such a terrible thing."

I tried to back off, though my sense of propriety was thoroughly shocked. "Why did you say that you didn't want the police to send Ted, then? Was he a terrible kisser or something? Did he try to take liberties with you?" My protective instincts were rising.

She shrugged. "Nothing like that. I don't know how I feel about him and if he shows up, he'll try and ask me to go on another date with him."

I had to grit my teeth not to scold Dora. She wasn't sure how she felt but she'd kissed him. What a foolish thing to do! After the way Ted had been looking at her, that would only make him more determined to see her again. It had knit the pair of them together when Dora might want to pull away.

To her great relief, the policeman who arrived was not Ted Grey. He took my statement and wrote everything down neatly in his little leather-bound notebook. Then he tipped his hat and walked to the door. Before he left, he turned to my aunt and said, "You might feel better if there's a man who can stay the night here. Do you have a brother or uncle in the area?"

Aunt Muriel clutched the neck of her dress and shook her head, looking as though she hadn't considered this and now had to check every shadow for a bad guy.

"I don't know whether you'd consider it or not," Gus stepped forward, "but I'd be happy to stay. I'd just be at home worrying about the two of you anyway. Besides, you've got a very comfortable sofa here."

The look of relief on Aunt Muriel's face was in humorous contrast to the worry that had been there last night when Gus had arrived. It told me that we'd be entertaining him another night and my spirits rose considerably.

Charlie, on the other hand, was not at all pleased. He glowered at us and I sighed inwardly. Boys sure had a way of complicating life.

CHAPTER TEN

D ora suggested that she ask their cook, Martha, to
make supper for us all. She offered to bring it over
and we'd have a dinner party right in the fern-filled dining
room at my aunt's house. Since that meant that she wouldn't
have to provide another big meal for our hungry guest, Aunt
Muriel agreed to the plan readily enough.

Gus announced that he wanted to go home and get
what he'd need to stay over another night as well as check in
with his boss. Once Gus left, Charlie relaxed. He also
needed to go in to his father's office to get some work done
but promised to return in time for supper.

My head was aching and I gave my excuses and went
up to lie down. Once alone, my mind kept whirling around
the morning's events. I hadn't had time to fully process it
while I was surrounded but now it came crashing down on
me. There was something so very frightening about being
attacked like that so close to my home. Would Hardy's men
actually be willing to enter Aunt Muriel's house in order to
silence me? The thought brought fresh panic washing over
me every time I was able to calm myself.

Was this how Jean had felt right before she died? She'd been strangled to death. Had her killer gotten his hands around her from the back? I wondered if she'd been surprised or if she'd been able to confront her attacker. Perhaps they'd argued before he grabbed her throat and squeezed the life out of her. Or had someone climbed out of the darkest shadows, stealthily crept up behind her, and had his hands on her before she knew he was even there?

For the first time, I knew a little of what Jean had felt the night she died. Whenever I'd ready mysteries before I'd had little patience for women who didn't fight back against their attackers. I understood now that fighting back against a man wasn't always enough. For the first time, I knew that if a man came into my house, he could hurt me and I might not be strong enough to stop him.

My hands shook, and I couldn't get warm enough, no matter how many quilts I piled on the bed. Finally, I knew I had to get my mind onto something else. I dug out another pair of thick wool socks and put them on over the pair I was already wearing. I slipped into my warmest sweater and then propped myself up against the pillows and reached for my book.

I'd already read all four of Agatha Christie's novels, but couldn't resist going back to them time and again. There was something so soothing about stepping into the world of Hercule Poirot, Tommy and Tuppence, or Colonel Race. The characters had become my friends and I loved getting caught up in the mystery, even though I now knew the endings by heart. If anything could get my mind off of the frightening events of the day, it was _The Mysterious Affair at Styles_. Despite my best efforts, my copy was beginning to look rather worn. Mother and Dad always gave me whichever newest novel was published for either my birthday or Christmas, jotting a short note inside the front cover.

Today it felt especially good to run my fingers over Dad's thin script which read, *"Happy birthday to my clever daughter – 1921."* Maybe if I touched the words long enough, some magic inside them would flow up through me and I would be as clever as Dad believed me to be. I would need every ounce of cleverness I could muster to solve this mystery.

Opening to the first page, I plunged greedily into the story, actively shutting off my mind to everything that had to do with real mystery and danger. Eventually, the terror that had gripped me eased completely and I found myself growing sleepy. Finally, I lay down and indulged in a delicious nap.

I woke in midafternoon and made my way downstairs. Aunt Muriel was knitting in her chair, her lips the thinnest of lines.

"Your friend, Dora, has been very high-handed today," she began, needles clicking ferociously.

"Oh?" I asked as I took my place and started my own knitting.

Aunt Muriel glared at me over the tops of her spectacles. "She's been in and out of this house half a dozen times. She moved my plants."

Ah, there it was. I hid my grin. "Where did she move them?"

"Into the sunroom. She didn't think there would be enough room in the dining room for five of us. I told her there would be, in no uncertain terms, but she wouldn't listen. I informed her that the sun is too intense in the sunroom but even that didn't stop her. If my ferns don't survive, I will hold her personally responsible."

Considering that it was early December and cloudy to boot, I wasn't worried about the plants. I had a feeling that I could best assuage Aunt Muriel by letting her get everything off her chest, so the afternoon moved at a sluggish pace while my aunt talked freely. She moved from the topic of Dora to how the milkman wasn't properly cleaning the bottles to the outrageous price of beef.

Dora's entrance through the kitchen door was like the singing of angels when the gates of heaven opened. The morning's headache hadn't survived my nap, though a fresh one was building due to my clenched teeth. We busied ourselves with spreading a tablecloth and setting five places at the dining room table. I had to admit that it was much easier to move around the room without the infernal plants everywhere.

We went and fetched the food and soon the house was filled with delicious smells. Both Gus and Charlie arrived and we had a merry time eating and ignoring Aunt Muriel's pointed comments. The conversation studiously avoided any mention of Jean Waldeck or the threats we'd stirred up.

Even cleaning up was great fun. My aunt went to the sitting room and the four of us young people washed and dried the dishes, swept the floor, and put everything away. Talk moved easily from which pictures we preferred to stories of hijinks we'd witnessed during grade school. Somehow it was revealed that I had once entered a prize-winning piglet in the county fair and the three found this very amusing. Their gentle teasing and curious questions made it seem all in good fun, though, and I found myself laughing at the story myself. Before we finished, the boys even moved all the plants back into the dining room, though there was much grinning and winking as they did so.

Finally, the hour grew late. Dora and Charlie left and

Aunt Muriel took herself up to bed. I turned to Gus as the quiet settled around us, feeling unsure what to do or say next.

"Do you want to play checkers?" he asked, and I gratefully agreed.

We set up the board at the kitchen table and I made a pot of coffee. We said little as we each planned our first moves and sipped at our cups.

"So, how are you enjoying life in Port Vernon?" Gus asked once we'd settled into the rhythm of the game.

"I never dreamed there would be so many mysteries to solve." I rubbed my forehead and sighed.

Gus gave me a curious look and I realized I wanted very much to tell him about everything that had happened at church. Soon, the game slowed to a stop as I filled him in on the strange food poisoning episodes.

"It isn't everyone," I summarized, "and it isn't the same people or even the same spot."

Gus's face was screwed up in concentration. "A different table at each supper is hit."

"With one exception, yes. Sylvester Young was sitting at the table next to the one where everyone was sick, and he also fell ill."

"Why would someone get up from his table and go to another table?" Gus mused.

"Why do you ask that?" I replied sharply. Something was beginning to grow clearer in my mind, though it was still a bit hazy.

"It seems to me that there must be something at a particular table that is making people sick. Whatever it is gets moved around and doesn't stay in one spot. Is there something that gets put out that isn't shared between tables?

Something that someone else might get up and use if he didn't have it at his table?"

My eyes grew wide and I snapped my fingers. "The salt and pepper shakers! Every table had its own and Mrs. Worth filled them in the kitchen. They would be used by one table each night and Sylvester Young might have borrowed one if his was empty."

"Why would only one of them be poisoned?" Gus asked, leaning forward eagerly.

I mulled that over. "Maybe the poisoner was interrupted. People are always coming in and out of the church. Of course, it's possible that it was accidental. I can't picture one of the little old ladies there wanting to hurt someone intentionally. The shakers would be emptied at different rates. If just one of them was a little low, it's possible that someone was merely topping up the single low shaker and grabbed the poison by mistake."

I pictured little Mrs. Worth with her thick glasses, clouded with fingerprint smudges. What if someone had put a poisonous substance back in the wrong place? What if it was right next to the salt or pepper and she'd picked it up without realizing it?

"I'll go to the church tomorrow and talk with the pastor. Gus, we might have solved this mystery!" I grinned at him.

"We're turning into regular detectives," he said, echoing my grin. "We just have to wrap up the Waldeck case and we can go into business."

We both had a good chuckle at that before returning our attention to the game.

∾

It was a pleasant surprise to find that Gus had awakened

early and gone to Wilma's Bakery for donuts. Aunt Muriel ate hers with a knife and fork so that the sugar coating didn't shed too far and wide over her neat cream-colored sweater.

A knock at the front door surprised us all and Aunt Muriel stalked in, ready to scold whoever was daring to interrupt her breakfast. She returned with a large bouquet of pink roses in a cut glass vase.

"These are for you, Ruby," she said in a clipped voice as she set them in the middle of the kitchen table. "What a waste of good money."

I blinked at the arrangement. Never in my life had I received flowers before, and these were gorgeous. Who could have sent them? And why? They were most definitely extravagant, but also very welcome at the same time.

"Read the card," Gus pointed, and I plucked the small white envelope from amid the full blooms.

"'*I hope you're feeling better today. Thought you could use a spot of color while you recover.*'" I read. "It's signed, '*Yours, Charlie.*'"

Gus gave me a knowing look which I ignored, leaning forward to smell the heady perfume the roses emitted.

"I've never received flowers before." I smiled and sat back.

"There are worse things than having a sugar daddy like Charlie Beaumont," Gus teased. "If you're not careful, it won't be long before you turn into a gold digger."

"Stop it," I ordered, and checked to see if my aunt understood that it was a joke.

"Well, I'd better be on my way," announced Gus as he pushed back from the table. "Thanks for the wonderful hospitality, Miss Barnes."

"Ruby, walk him to the door," she ordered.

I followed our guest as he found the bag he'd brought from home and then pulled on his coat and hat.

"Thank you for staying over," I remembered to say, though I was flustered from receiving the flowers. "That was very kind of you. I know both Aunt Muriel and I slept better with you here."

"No sweat," he grinned. Then he lowered his voice and said, "I'll keep asking around about you-know-what. If I hear anything, I'll let you know."

"Thanks," I said, and opened the front door.

"See you around, cookie." Gus winked at me and strolled out the door.

CHAPTER ELEVEN

As I hurried through Aunt Muriel's shopping later that morning, I reflected on why I hadn't told Gus about the large bank deposit. Mother had always taught me that talking about money was vulgar. A person's finances were a personal thing and the church's finances were private as well as sacred. I supposed it was just habit that I kept such things quiet.

Aunt Muriel had finally decided that I was trustworthy enough to do her shopping. She was so scrupulous that this endeavor involved visiting two different green grocers, three butchers, and the bakery on the far side of town. I'd trailed after her on numerous occasions and learned everything that she had to teach me about the tricky endeavor. However, I had a feeling that the handing over of this chore had more to do with my aunt avoiding a long walk than with my capabilities.

It was very cold. The wind was spiteful and determined. Tiny snowflakes sought out every bit of skin and delighted in melting icily on my flesh. Thanks to my aunt, I had a large selection of knitted hats, mittens, and mufflers to choose from. Though far from fashionable, they were very warm. If I pulled down the edge of the stocking cap, I could get it to cover my eyebrows. Then I was able to wrap two scarves around my neck and bury my chin in them. Only my eyes and nose peeked out from between the rows of itchy wool and thus the vindictive winter had the smallest of available targets to use to torment me.

Nevertheless, by the time I returned home,

I was frozen through. Aunt Muriel opened packages and bags while I made a cup of strong, hot tea. I felt as though I was a student standing in front of the examination board. She clucked and sighed and I got a few stern glances, but on the whole she wasn't too unhappy about my morning's work.

"The Beaumont children were over earlier. They would like to speak with you as soon as you are available."

I suppressed a giggle at six-foot-tall Charlie being referred to as a child and instead smiled hopefully.

Aunt Muriel looked over the groceries which were scattered on the sideboard. She sighed. "You may go now. I'll see to putting these away. It's a delicate procedure that must be done exactly to my specifications." Which implied that I would surely muff it.

Considering that I had to go back out into the cold, I jumped to my feet with a great deal of enthusiasm. I didn't bother to bundle up too much and most certainly ignored my aunt's call to put on a hat. I wasn't sure how I felt about him yet, but I didn't want Charlie seeing me with hair fresh from being flattened under a stocking cap.

I tucked my head down and made my way to the church, hoping to wrap up my business there quickly and then make my way to the Beaumont's. The church's front door was open and I hurried downstairs, wanting to look through the cupboards myself before talking to Pastor Mason.

The basement of the church was divided into two sections. There was the larger meeting room which was used for all meetings and get-togethers that weren't appropriate for the sanctuary above. The kitchen was at the far end of the room. I hurried over, my heart beginning to pick up its pace.

Once I stepped into the kitchen, I flipped the switch and the naked bulb in the ceiling popped on with an electric whir. I hurried to the cupboards and opened them, searching for the containers of salt and pepper.

There! Two squat cardboard cylinders stood together. The label of one read "salt" and the other read "pepper." I pulled them down and then examined their neighbors. Baking soda, baking powder, no, no—they wouldn't make anyone sick. I paused and pulled out a large box of soap flakes, then put it aside. It was too large to be mistaken for the containers of salt or pepper.

Once that box was out of the way, I could see to the back of the cupboard. Tucked into the very darkest corner was a round cylinder similar in size to the containers in question. I bit my lip and pulled it out, hoping that my suspicions were about to be confirmed.

"Ace Wasp Killer," I read, and gave a triumphant shout.

Almost dropping it in my eagerness, I placed it on the counter and ran through the meeting room and up the stairs to the pastor's office.

"Miss Martin!" He looked up in surprise when I barreled through his door. "What on earth is the matter?"

"I know what happened! I've figured out why people are getting sick!"

Pastor Mason's eyebrows rose. "Indeed?"

"Come with me." I spun on my heel and could hardly keep myself from running back down to the kitchen. Fortunately, the reverend was every bit as eager to see what I'd discovered.

"Mrs. Worth is always given the task of filling the salt and pepper shakers. You know that she can't see well, even with her spectacles." I waited for his nod before continuing, "My friend pointed out that because the people who grow ill are typically at the same table, whatever is making them sick must be something that is moved from table to table at each event."

Pastor Mason's face lit up with understanding. "The salt and pepper cellars!"

I nodded and pointed to the cupboard. "I wondered if Mrs. Worth might have filled one of the salt or pepper shakers with something by mistake. I came here this morning to see if my hunch was correct. This was pushed into the back corner."

Heart pounding with excitement, I held up the container of wasp killer.

"Good heavens!" Pastor Mason took it from my hands and stared at it. "There's arsenic in wasp killer. No wonder people were so ill!"

He opened it and we peered in. The wasp killer was made up of thin black curling strings. Even though they wouldn't be mistaken for pepper if they were shaken onto food, they were potent enough to make the remaining pepper that did come out dangerous.

"And you say it was in the back corner?" The pastor was looking at me with such relief that I couldn't help smiling at him.

"Yes. My guess is that someone used it back in the summer and put it here by mistake. Someone took it down in September and Mrs. Worth used it. After that, it might not have been used, but the damage was done. Over time, it was pushed back as other items were used."

"Thank the Lord. Ruby, you've helped us tremendously! I'll make certain all the pepper cellars are cleaned and their contents disposed of. We need to find a different place to keep such a dangerous item." He shook his head and led the way back upstairs.

I was so elated that the mystery was solved that I fairly floated all the way to the Beaumont's.

"Hello, Martha," I called as I breezed into the kitchen.

The cook returned my greeting, calling hello over her shoulder as I hurried up to Dora's room. My friend was angrily hanging up clothes when I entered her room. She slammed a dress into the closet and scowled at it then turned to me. Instantly, her frown evaporated and she grinned ruefully.

"Mother said that if I didn't hang up the clothes I already have, she'll stop buying me new ones. I think it's a bluff, but I don't want to test her. Vogue had a darling layout of spring frocks and I'll simply die if I don't have one for the summer parties."

"Aunt Muriel said you needed to see me," I prompted as I divested myself of my outside clothes. The glow from solving the church's mystery couldn't be dampened easily. Even Dora's mess and her dramatic ways couldn't spoil my good mood.

"Oh, that's right. Let me get Charlie." And Dora scampered out of the room.

Before I had the chance to step over and hang up more than three of Dora's dresses, she was back with her brother in tow. Charlie sat on the bench and leaned back, resting his elbows on Dora's vanity. Dora perched on the end of the bed, not bothering to tell me to stop cleaning or even making a pretense of helping me complete her chore.

"What's going on?" I asked over my shoulder. I didn't mind putting clothes away and the large pile of discarded garments in Dora's room always called to me to come and tidy it.

"We have a plan," Dora said in a serious voice.

I paused and cocked my head. "A plan about what, exactly?"

"We need to know if our father is a drug lord." I would have laughed at Dora's dramatic words, but knew that, this time, she meant every one of them.

"I suppose I can understand that," I said slowly. "What is the plan?"

Charlie spun one of Dora's bangles around on his finger. He was working very hard at appearing nonchalant, I observed, and began to grow concerned. "We've been through Dad's office here at the house and we didn't find anything helpful. To be frank, we didn't really expect him to keep evidence that he was running drugs in his home. We figured that if we could get into his office downtown and go through things there, we'd find what we're looking for."

"Of course, you might not find anything if he's innocent," I pointed out.

"Sure, that's what we're hoping for," Charlie amended hastily.

"How are you going to get into his office?" I asked as I shook out a sapphire-blue day dress.

"Well, we sort of need your help for that," Dora said slowly.

"My help?" My stomach began to fill with dread.

Dora hurried to get it out. "We want you to go to

Daddy's office and make it sound like you're needing some financial help."

I stared from one of them to the other.

"I don't understand. Why would I ask your father for help?" I was completely lost.

Charlie's jaw was clenched and Dora looked too bright as she said, "Our father is the sort of man who likes to help pretty young women."

I shook my head, confused.

"He helps them in exchange for certain ... favors. Personal favors," Dora said grimly.

My eyes widened as I cottoned on. "Oh, no. I couldn't ever suggest such a thing!"

"You don't have to suggest anything. You just go into Daddy's office and tell him that your aunt is struggling with money and that you're afraid he'll evict her. Look at him with big, sad eyes and he'll come up with the plan all on his own."

I gaped. How awful that Dora and Charlie suspected such a thing about their own father. It was one thing to know that Mr. Beaumont had a mistress and another thing to know that he was a wolf who would prey on any young woman. No wonder Charlie didn't want to turn into his father.

Dora took my silence for assent. "Once you're in Daddy's office, Charlie will ask Daddy to help him with something in another part of the building and you'll be alone for a few minutes. You can look through his papers and see if there's any mention of the *Baker's Dozen* or Louis Hardy or dope."

"No," I refused flatly. "Absolutely not."

Charlie pushed to his feet and came over to me. "Dora or I would do it, but Dad would be suspicious. Dora has absolutely no interest in the company and hasn't visited since she was a kid. It only makes sense that I'm the one who calls him away. I'm working on a project there that he's overseeing. We just need someone who has a real reason to go in and see him at the office instead of here at the house. And when he comes back, you can announce that you made a huge mistake in coming and run out of the room. It's the sort of thing Dad will expect a weak female to do."

I shook my head frantically. "You said that your father is out of his office all the time. Why not wait until then and sneak in yourself? You won't need me."

Dora stood up and came over to me. Taking my hand, she implored, "Please, Ruby? We can't bear to wait any longer. It might be a week before Daddy's out of his office and then Charlie would have to steal the key from his secretary. You have to help us right away. You can't imagine how awful it is to imagine that your own father is a criminal and maybe a murderer. Charlie and I have to know the truth."

I gulped and looked from Charlie's carefully stoic face to Dora's tearful one and felt my resolve crumble.

Dora had gone to the pictures too many times, I grumbled to myself as I walked into the Beaumont office building later that afternoon. She'd insisted that I return home to put on a different dress. Waifish yet attractive was the look we were trying to achieve, she'd explained. I was quite sure she'd gotten the idea from Mary Pickford or Louise Brooks.

Then she'd given me a delicate touch of makeup and declared that my long hair pinned at the nape of my neck was just right for the part. I found that mildly offensive, but held the thought in. Dora also decided that wearing her brown tam would be better since it set off my eyes and didn't look too flashy.

Now, my heart thundered in my chest as I strode up to the receptionist's desk. "I'd like to speak with Mr. Beaumont," I said in a shaky voice.

"Do you have an appointment?" the woman asked in a suppressive voice.

"No, but I'm friends with his daughter and I believe that he'll want to see me." I saw understanding in her eyes and it made me squirm. I was only making the vaguest of suggestions that I would consider a tryst with him and it was still enough to make me feel dirty.

I was instructed to sit in the waiting area while a boy was sent up to check on my request. Within a few minutes, the boy was back and I was given directions up to the senior director's office. As I went, I was too aware of the eyes of everyone in the office watching me go. I could almost hear their thoughts as I passed. It made me want to turn and run all the way back to Aunt Muriel's.

Fortunately, Charlie was standing in his office doorway when I walked by and he gave me a bracing nod. My resolve bucked up and I lifted my chin. I was helping my friends prove that their father was innocent. That was a cause worth this emotional turmoil.

Mr. Beaumont was quick to usher me into his office. He indicated a chair for me sit in and then reclined in the chair next to mine. I'd expected to have his large desk between us and was momentarily thrown off by the seating arrangement. Then I mentally shook my head and focused on the task at hand.

I gulped and examined him. He was like an older version of Charlie, except that there was a darkness in him that wasn't in his son. There was no spark of happiness anywhere in him. Was he behind the drug ring? Was this what happened to a man who was willing to commit those sorts of horrible crimes?

I schooled my features and tried to look shy and appealing. There was little chance that I was successful but Mr. Beaumont didn't seem put off by my expression, so I sighed and said, "I'm sorry to burst in on you like this, but I really don't know who else to go to."

"What's wrong, my dear?" His face was full of concern. It was almost endearing.

"I've come to realize that my aunt is in a difficult situation. Financially, I mean," I stumbled on. "The money her brother has been sending her is no longer enough to cover her costs. I'm afraid that she might lose the ability to afford the rent on the house." I batted my eyelashes at him in a way that I hoped was winsome.

A subtle look of confident triumph flitted in his eyes briefly and I knew that he'd bought the story Dora had concocted. She knew her father well, as it turned out. "What is it exactly that you are hoping I'll do for you?" he asked.

I was cornered like a mouse in front of a hungry cat. There was nothing for me to do but suggest that he and I strike up a mutually beneficial arrangement. Dora had told me just what to say at the house in case I had to speak the words, but now I found myself choking on them.

The knock on the door was almost enough to undo me completely. I started violently and gaped in horror at whoever would enter the room and surely know that I was lying. Charlie stepped in and I was sure that I'd never been so glad to see someone before in my life.

"Oh, hello, Ruby," Charlie acted surprised to see me. "What are you doing here?"

"She and I have some business to attend to about the house her aunt is renting from me. It's no concern of yours, Charles," Mr. Beaumont said briskly.

"I've been working on the Dilworth project. There are two ways we can go at this point, but I want you to weigh in on it. Would you mind letting me steal Dad away for just a few minutes, Ruby?" Charlie bypassed his father and I gave my assent quickly.

Mr. Beaumont had to go with his son or look rude. Luckily for us, he wasn't the sort of man to lose face in front of a young woman he was hoping to seduce. "I'll be back shortly," he said to me as he stood and clapped Charlie on the shoulder.

The moment the door closed behind them, I jumped to my feet and rushed to the desk. Filing cabinets lined the walls but Charlie had speculated that it was unlikely he'd have private documents about illegal activities there. Apparently, Mr. Beaumont had a fleet of stenographers and secretaries who were in and out of those files daily. The only truly private place in the room was the desk.

I pulled open the top drawer, looking over the array of fountain pens, ink, and general clutter. There was nothing out of the ordinary there. Another drawer held pads of paper and a ledger filled with abbreviations that meant nothing to me. It was possible that this was incriminating, but I had no way of knowing for sure. Besides, trying to smuggle a ledger out of the office was beyond my abilities.

Seconds were hurrying past and I couldn't leave any drawers untouched. I promised myself I'd make up my mind about the ledger later, if I had time. Perhaps Charlie could come back when his father was gone and look through it.

The largest drawer of all held hanging file folders and I

flipped through each quickly. From everything I scanned, I came to quickly understand that the Beaumont business was made up of many smaller corporations. I saw a construction company, a utility company, something having to do with mining in West Virginia, and a variety of stores scattered throughout southeastern Michigan. Nothing out of the ordinary.

I closed the door with a sigh. Did this mean that Mr. Beaumont was not involved with the drug ring? Just because I hadn't found anything that said he was didn't mean he was innocent. Even though this might be seen as good news, I doubted that Charlie and Dora would be too relieved.

Out of desperation, I searched the items on the top of the desk. Nothing there was holding some nefarious information. As a final thought, I lifted the blotter and was stunned when a note on decorative paper was revealed lying hidden underneath. It took me a moment to understand what I was seeing: this was no work memorandum.

I picked up the letter and replaced the blotter. It was most definitely a woman's stationery, the sort that she would save for intimate, romantic notes. It wasn't my business, and was probably not at all related to drug smuggling, but I unfolded it anyway.

My eyes scanned to the bottom and deciphered the big, brash signature. At that exact moment, the door opened and Mr. Beaumont stepped into the room.

I stared up at him in horror, not knowing what it was that frightened me most: being caught reading his private letter or the fact that it was signed, *"All my love, Jean Waldeck."*

CHAPTER TWELVE

The moment stretched as we stood facing off. I was sure that Mr. Beaumont would fly across the room and strangle me with his bare hands. When he calmly reached behind him and closed the office door, I knew I was right. There was no other exit, though I searched for one frantically.

"It's not what it looks like, Miss Martin," he said. Mr. Beaumont spoke slowly, as though trying to calm a wild animal. He began to walk towards me with careful, even steps. I noticed his hands, held out in front of him, were trembling.

"This is a love letter from Jean Waldeck. I take it that you are her *'Darling Clare,'*" I read the salutation from the top.

He stopped short and looked away as though collecting his emotions. When he spoke, his voice was breathy. "I don't know if you'll believe me or not, but Jean and I were involved in a short affair a few months back. She called it off and moved on to Louis Hardy. I was devastated and couldn't bear to dispose of that letter."

I examined the man standing in front of me. He certainly looked remorseful. Was it an act or was it genuine?

Mr. Beaumont lifted a hand to his face and rubbed it as though he was exhausted to his very bones. "When I heard that she was killed, I was terrified that someone would find out that she and I were involved. It would certainly give me a good reason to want her dead. Still, I couldn't destroy it.

"You have to believe me, Miss Martin, I did not kill Jean. I was heartbroken, but I didn't want her dead."

My terror that I was about to die was ebbing and I read over the letter. It was playful and teasing enough that I could understand why a man like Mr. Beaumont would want to be involved with such a woman.

He sank onto one of the chairs and wiped at his eyes. "I can't believe she's gone. She was so full of life. It was the happiest weeks I've had in a long time. You don't understand the pressure I'm under. I have hundreds of employees who depend on me for their livelihoods. My children depend on me to provide a good living for them. My wife wants me to give her a life that makes everyone in Port Vernon envious. Jean just wanted me."

He seemed so sad and broken that I took a gamble. "Mr. Beaumont, I've been looking into Jean's death with the help of Charlie and Dora. We've come to learn that someone in this town is running a large drug operation and it's possible that this person was behind Jean's murder."

I sat across from him and watched his face carefully. He seemed surprised to hear that we'd been digging into the mystery of Jean's death but not about the drugs. "Do you know who is bringing drugs across from Canada and selling them in town?"

Dora's father shook his head and sighed. "It's common knowledge that there's some high-ranking person running things. Unfortunately, the only one who ever has access to that person is Louis Hardy. I warned Jean to stay away from him." He gripped his hands together for a moment as the pain washed over him.

"Why are you selling your boat?" I asked even though it was none of my business and unrelated to the case.

"Jean loved to go out on the water. I'd planned to sell it after she left me but once I learned of her death, I decided I'd keep it as a reminder of happier times."

If he was acting, he was better than John Barrymore. Not knowing what else to say, I got to my feet and said good-bye. As I closed the door, I looked back at Dora's father and saw him sitting with his head in his hands, completely bereft.

The lack of evidence, Jean's letter, and their father's denial were enough to convince both Dora and Charlie that he was not a drug smuggler. They both looked as though a great weight had been lifted from them, though they were dismayed to hear that he'd been involved with Jean.

"No wonder she was so smug at that party," Dora hissed, punching one fist into her other palm. "She'd been involved with my own father!"

Dora thanked me half a dozen times for clearing her father's name and enfolded me in a tight embrace before I was allowed to return home for supper. I found that I was glad that I'd gone along with this plan. The weight of worry that their father was involved in something so evil had clearly been weighing painfully on both of the older Beaumont children.

Even Aunt Muriel's lecture on the importance of

wearing long underwear from October through the month of April couldn't dampen my high spirits. In one day I'd solved the problem at the church and helped Charlie and Dora clear their father's name.

I nodded along as my aunt spoke, hoping that she wouldn't check to see if I was wearing my long underwear once spring arrived. We got through the meal in mostly companionable conversation and the kitchen was soon tidied.

We settled in for another long, dull evening of knitting. I longed for a radio to keep us company but knew that Aunt Muriel was not likely to ever splurge on such a luxury. She would enjoy it if we had one, but that was irrelevant in view of her thrifty ways. I sighed hopelessly as I took in the sock I was supposed to be knitting. Somehow, no matter how hard I tried, whatever I was knitting always ended up lumpy.

The knock on the kitchen door was a very welcome interruption. I put my knitting down and practically jumped out of my seat. In all likelihood, it was probably Dora or Charlie. Even so, remembering the attack from the previous day, I peeked cautiously through the lace curtain, rather than throwing the door open as usual, and saw Gus standing there.

My curiosity rose as I opened the door. He beckoned me to step outside with a single finger. I glanced over my shoulder before wrapping my sweater more tightly against the cold and joining him on the back step.

"There's a shipment coming in tonight on the *Baker's Dozen*. A friend of mine overheard some of Hardy's men talking about it at a joint down by the dock. I was thinking that we could go and see if we witness anything that we can take to the police. I don't know about you, but I'm ready to find some piece of evidence that we can use to put an end to our involvement."

I couldn't agree more. "Is there a good place to hide? I don't want another run-in with Hardy's goons."

"The boat docks at the same pier every time. It's close to one of the warehouses. There are always lots of crates stacked up. If we leave soon, we should be able to get there in time to build a good hiding place before Hardy shows up, if there isn't one already in place."

"Would you mind if we brought Dora along?" I asked. "I think we might be glad to have one more person."

Gus considered this. "If you think it's a good idea, cookie, I'm all for it. Can you get away from your aunt?"

"I'll tell her that you asked me to go for a walk in the snow."

"Good idea," he nodded.

We stepped inside and Gus worked his charms on Aunt Muriel while I added a second layer of long underwear, my thickest stockings, and an extra pair of sweaters. By the time I got back downstairs, Aunt Muriel was putting one of her handmade knit stocking hats on Gus' head and wrapping one of her itchy, but very warm, scarves around his neck. Once I received the same treatment, we were allowed to leave.

Our next stop was at the Beaumont's, where Dora eagerly ran up to her room to pile on the layers, and in under 10 minutes we were making our way to the docks. We talked over our plan of action and then huddled close to try and keep warm.

∾

This side of town was far from affluent. Between the train yard and shipyard, it was rough and industrial. The houses that hadn't been knocked down to make way for industry were old and run down. We passed a few buildings that were clearly hiding speakeasies from the men in patched coats and trousers flowing in and out of these establishments, some already plastered.

Gus led us to the dark side of a warehouse which faced an empty pier. He gave me and Dora instructions and together we shoved wooden crates into both a respectable hiding spot and windbreak. The spot was a good one, giving us a clear view of where the ship would dock and unload its cargo. It was also close enough to the warehouse door that we would be able to see the men well when they turned on some lights inside.

We settled back to wait, pressed together in the huddle. Dora was struggling to stay still. She kept craning her neck to peek around the edge of the warehouse at the closest speakeasy and moaning with longing.

"Do you have any idea how much warmer we would be if we had a little hooch?" she nagged.

"Dora, we can't. If we get called to testify about what we see, we can't have been drinking. Any defense lawyer worth his salt would rip our testimony to shreds," I explained again.

The time dragged by and my feet became increasingly numb. The cold seemed to soak through the layers I'd put on without any regard for the effort I'd put forth. Gus, though, was solid as a statue. Whether he didn't notice the cold or was too tough to shiver, I wasn't sure.

The sound of a car pulling up behind us drew our attention. We looked over and I was surprised to see Charlie's shiny gray car parking. He climbed out and walked into the building as though he regularly did so. I sighed and shook my head. After all the talking we'd done, I'd hoped that he wasn't so keen on drinking.

"Oh, Charlie just went in," Dora said, excitement in her voice. "I think I'll go and get a little liquid courage. The two of you will have to do all the testifying in court. See you soon!"

And before we could tell her not to, Dora popped up and sashayed across the road, disappearing through the door. I hit my fist against my leg in frustration.

"Careful there," Gus teased. "Don't do yourself any permanent damage."

"I can't believe Dora left us," I groused. Gus raised an eyebrow and I rolled my eyes. "I mean, I can believe it, I'm just angry that she would do that."

He shook his head in disbelief. "That's the thing about rich people I don't understand. They've never been cold or hungry or lacked for anything. Still, they act like their lives have been so difficult. What sorrows do those two have to drink away? I know a fellow whose old man lost a leg and an arm in the Great War. My friend had to drop out of school when he was twelve so he could support his family. With him, his mother, and two of his sisters working, they can almost make ends meet. I would understand why he would want to get sloshed."

"The Beaumonts have plenty of sorrows of their own," I replied, thinking of their father. "The thing I don't understand is why people like drinking so much. Alcohol tastes awful. It makes you do stupid things. And then you feel horrible the next day. Is all that worth a few hours' escape?"

"Sometimes things get so lonely or so hard that you'll do

anything to not feel it," Gus said wistfully. "When you're with a group of people and you're all laughing and drinking, you can pretend that they're your best mates and you're all having a swell time instead of being alone."

"Do you ever feel lonely?" I asked, worried.

Gus was quiet for so long that I thought he wouldn't answer. Finally, he said, "All I've got left is a sister. No folks. Just one sister who's busy with her husband and their new baby. I have some friends, but I go home to a one-room apartment I rent from an old lady. I work three jobs regularly and, at the end of the day, I don't know that I've done anything worth doing. I just go from day to day, hoping that someday it'll be better."

"If you could have any job, what would you like to do?" I asked, saddened.

"You'll probably laugh," he said carefully.

"I won't, I promise."

Gus scratched his chin. "I'd like to write a book."

"That's not funny at all," I exclaimed. "I think you would make a wonderful writer."

"Really? What makes you think I'd be good? You've never read a single word I've written." His eyes challenged me playfully.

I thought that over. "You read people well. I think you'd be able to write great characters because you understand what makes people tick and how to win them over."

His expression became pleasantly surprised. "No kidding. You think that?"

"I do," I nodded. "Do you like to read? I read somewhere once that in order to be a great writer, you have to be a great reader."

"I read whenever I can. I haven't been able to have a library card since I was a kid and my pops accidentally threw my book in the fire. I tried to explain to the librarian but she cast a kitten and threw me out." He smirked at the memory. "Maybe once she finally retires, I'll be able to get the new one to let me borrow a book or two. But this one's already about 112 and she's not going anywhere soon."

"Well, if you can be careful, you're welcome to borrow any book I have," I offered.

"Thanks, cookie. I might just take you up on that."

We fell into companionable silence, our arms pressed together, and watched the water. After a while, the sound of footsteps behind us made us freeze in place. To our relief, Dora and Charlie appeared.

"You didn't think I'd let you all have an adventure without me," Charlie said good-naturedly.

"Welcome to the fun," Gus quipped. "You're welcome to share in our icy toes and runny noses any time."

No sooner had the two Beaumonts settled in beside us than lights across the water heralded the coming of a boat.

"This is it," Gus whispered.

We all sat up straighter, making sure we had a good view. Sure enough, the boat docked at the pier right in front of us and a handful of shifty-looking fellows began unloading the cargo.

"Hey, that's one of the guys who jumped me in the alley," Gus pointed. "I recognize his coat and hat."

"Do you think that's enough reason to get the police?" I asked, excitement rising.

Charlie considered that. "I think it is. Gus, why don't you take my car and go for the cops? I'd go, but I've been drinking."

"Are you sure you're okay without me?" Gus moved to a crouch.

We nodded that we were and he accepted Charlie's

offer with a handshake and a firm nod.

"Don't do anything stupid," he whispered before slinking away.

CHAPTER THIRTEEN

We knelt in the darkness, our faces pressed against the cracks between the crates. Hardy's men finished unloading the boat and hauling the crates into the warehouse. There was no sign of Hardy himself, though we examined every face, hoping to spot him. The boat's captain and extra crew members finished tying up the boat and headed across to the speakeasy across the road.

After Hardy's men went into the warehouse with the final load, the three of us sat back.

"What do we do now?" Dora voiced my thoughts.

I chewed my lip. "If the police come, they won't have anything to go on other than the fact that we saw some men carrying crates inside. It doesn't necessarily link the smuggled goods to Louis Hardy or Jean Waldeck."

"We don't know what's in the crates either," Charlie pointed out. "If it's nothing but imitation fur coats, they won't get more than a slap on the wrist. And if it's panther sweat, the cops will probably be willing to keep their mouths shut in exchange for a few bottles."

"I wish we hadn't sent Gus," I moaned. "We've got to

find out if there's something illegal going on here. Something definite that links Louis Hardy to the drug ring."

Dora whispered, "Well, let's sneak in and see what we find." When Charlie and I just stared at Dora, she grew indignant. "Golly gee, don't look at me like that! This could be our best chance of finding some dope and catching Jean's killer."

She was right. I'd wanted to go in but had been hesitant to voice it. It was ridiculously dangerous for the three of us to sneak into the warehouse where a murderous dope smuggler kept his stash of goods. Still, if we didn't do it, the police would be no closer to finding the man who killed Jean.

Thankfully, Charlie came to the same conclusion. "All right. Let's go, but stay behind me. And if I say to run, you vamoose."

"And how," Dora nodded fervently.

Charlie stood up, pressed himself against the wall, and crept to the door. He flattened himself in the shadows and leaned forward so that only his head peeked around the edge. The moment stretched until Charlie looked back at where Dora and I shivered behind the crates and beckoned for us to follow him.

We bent over as though we might be seen from above and hightailed it over to where Charlie stood. After a few heartbeats, he slid around the edge of the door with Dora and me right behind.

Thankfully, there were piles of crates everywhere. It took little effort to dart into a shadowy corner and watch the men handle the new arrivals. They were using crowbars and hammers to pull the lids off the wooden boxes. Coarse laughter reached us from time to time as they grunted and pulled. Once all the crates were opened, the men sat back. They appeared to be waiting for someone. The minutes stretched. Finally, one man checked his wristwatch and then hitched a thumb back towards the speakeasy. This suggestion was met with enthusiasm and the group tromped past us and noisily made their way across the street.

We waited until we were sure that we were alone before creeping out from our hiding place and scurrying over to the crates.

"Go fast," Charlie urged. "They are definitely expecting someone who could arrive at any moment."

I moved to the nearest crate and began to paw at the straw filling out of the way. My hand brushed against a bottle and I pulled it out to where I could read the label in the dim light cast by a few naked bulbs high above us. It was gin with a Canadian label. No surprise there. A further search of the crate revealed only more bottles of alcohol.

"I've got whiskey over here," Charlie called. "Ruby, what about you?"

"Gin." I moved on to the next crate.

"That's funny," Dora called. "Why would they be smuggling plaster ornaments?"

Charlie and I both looked up at her. She lifted a very ugly cat statue out of the crate and held it up to us.

"That can't be worth more than a dollar," I said, stumped. "Why would they bother to bring that over? Are you sure that crate is with this shipment?"

"The lid's off, and it's surrounded by the other crates," Dora shrugged. "I can't imagine anyone ever buying this thing. Who would want one in their house?" She shuddered dramatically.

Charlie snapped his fingers and practically jumped over to his sister's side. "I'll bet you anything that the cat isn't the valuable part." He took it from Dora and cracked it on the side of the crate. The cat's smirking face broke in two and

Charlie pulled the statue open the rest of the way. There was nothing inside and my shoulders dropped. I hadn't realized how much I'd hoped that Charlie's hunch was correct. Dora, however, grabbed another statue and smashed it gleefully on the ground. Once again, there was nothing.

They made their way through half a dozen statues and I was about to tell them to stop when Charlie gave a shout and wrenched a statue open, then held the two halves up for us to see.

I gasped as white packets fell to the ground. "They're hiding the drugs in the statues! That's brilliant. Even if they were searched, they couldn't find anything."

Dora reached down and picked up one of the packets. She held it up to the light. "What is this? Cocaine?"

"Probably," Charlie nodded.

The three of us looked at each other excitedly. We'd done it! We'd found how the dope was being smuggled into the country. It was enough to justify the police coming. Even if it couldn't be tied to Louis Hardy, the police would be on the right track.

"We need to get out of here," I said, my common sense breaking through my excitement. "Dora, pack up that cat and some of the packets. Then let's go."

The two Beaumonts looked around until they found a burlap sack, tossed in the fragments of cat, and Dora added the packet she'd picked up. Then we turned and hurried back towards the warehouse door and freedom, not bothering to hide among the crates piled around the edges. We were only a few steps from getting away when Louis Hardy himself rounded the corner with two big thugs in tow.

We froze, horrified. Hardy needed no more than a few heartbeats to assess the situation. He whipped a pistol out from his belt and ordered his men to grab us. With the gun trained on Charlie, neither Dora nor I dared to try and make a run for it.

"My, my," he clucked with an evil laugh, "if it isn't little Charlie Beaumont and his sister. Are you looking for something? I'm surprised to see you sneaking around my warehouse. Your father is rich enough that you shouldn't need to steal booze from me."

My heart leapt momentarily. If Hardy just thought we were lifting a few bottles, we might escape unharmed. There was a chance we'd get out of this all right.

"We know all about you and Jean," Dora exclaimed, and my heart sank.

Hardy's face sharpened and he stalked closer to Dora. "Is that so? What is it, exactly, that you think you know?"

I willed Dora to keep her mouth shut. *Please, please, for once in your life, don't say anything!*

Dora seemed determined to bluff it out. "We know that you killed Jean Waldeck and that you're smuggling dope in from Canada on your boat. We even know who you're working for!"

He opened the burlap sack. We watched Hardy thoughtfully run a finger over the cat statue and extract the packet of white powder. He cocked an eyebrow at us, his previous joviality turning sinister.

"Do you? You seem awfully anxious to spill your secrets, considering that I'm supposed to be a killer." I held my breath as Hardy examined us shrewdly. His eyes settled on my face and he said, "You're Ruby Martin, aren't you? You're Gus Jones' girlfriend. He's been nosing about my business and you've been helping him. I was informed that you two were asking Jeannie's brother questions about me."

My stomach dropped. This was not good. Despite my fear, my heart registered being called Gus's girlfriend and gave a tiny flutter. I scolded my foolish heart and turned my attention resolutely to the problem at hand.

"I thought that sending the pair of you a message would be enough to get you off my case. I guess I wasn't firm enough. A few cracked ribs and a good scare just don't do as much as they used to." He shook his head. "Fellows, let's take them up to the office."

The thugs produced leather thongs from their pockets, barked at us to hold our hands out in front of us, and tied our wrists. When Charlie looked as though he was going to fight back, Hardy cocked his pistol and snarled, "I dare you to try it. One wrong move and you can tell Jean hello for us."

Dora and I exchanged terrified looks. The men pushed us towards the stairs and we stumbled up. Hardy ordered that we be tied to chairs while he telephoned someone he called "the boss."

We were pushed into rickety wooden chairs which lined one wall, Hardy's gun trained on us as he and his goons spoke quietly in the doorway. Dora, Charlie, and I exchanged frightened looks. We were in deep trouble and we knew it. My mind moved frantically through escape plans, each more unlikely to work than the next.

My eyes scanned the room repeatedly as I sat there plotting, yet I failed to initially pay attention to the details of the warehouse office. Slowly, I began to register what I was seeing. It was full of battered filing cabinets and splintery wooden desks. There were crates with their hay cushioning poking out between the slats.

One desk, however, stood out from the others, and as I grew accustomed to my fear, I examined it more carefully. The desk was of finer quality than the rest. It had a padded chair behind it and its top was so tidy that it would have been welcome in Aunt Muriel's house. A single cat statute sat keeping watch over the thick account book, blotter, and ink pot.

I can't tell you why that desk so fascinated me. Perhaps it was the panic of finding myself facing death that caused me to be unable to look away. Maybe I was losing my grip on reality and focusing instead on something that wasn't terrifying.

A car door slammed outside and my heart leapt.

"It's the boss," one of the goons growled.

"Keep an eye on these three," Hardy ordered, hanging up the receiver without having reached his party. "We'll go down and explain the situation." Hardy tucked the pistol back into his jacket and he and the other thug clattered down the hallway and to the stairs.

The flunky who remained to guard us pulled out a knife and waved it at us. "Don't try anything."

I pursed my lips. By the time Hardy returned with the boss, we'd be as good as dead. There would be no hope for escape by then. A knife was just as deadly as a gun, but one man was far less difficult than four.

Catching Dora's eye, I lifted an eyebrow and nodded my head towards the thug. Understanding lit in her face and she began to wiggle in her seat.

"Sit still," the man frowned at Dora.

"Gee, I'm dying to ... you know ... go." She smiled apologetically. "I'd hate to have an accident right here."

"Do it. See if I care." The thug shrugged and began cleaning his fingernails with his knife.

"Dora, you're such a baby," I jumped in and scolded her. "I told you to take care of that before we left home. You never think!"

"I like that! It was your dumb idea to come in here and look around. If anyone's to blame, it's you!" Dora whined.

I got to my feet and pointed an accusing finger at Dora, my hands still tied in front of me. "You're the one who drinks gin, not me. And you're the one who wanted me to investigate this in the first place. I never would have done half of these stupid things if it wasn't for you!"

Dora popped up and began hollering at me. I yelled back and Charlie got up, trying to push us apart. The goon began to tell us to quiet down and when he came over, his knife wasn't threatening us any longer.

Moving fast, Charlie grabbed the man's hand and dodged his blows while I wrenched the knife away. Then Charlie had his hands full holding off the thug as I cut Dora's bonds and then she cut mine.

Charlie took a fist to the head and slumped to the floor. Dora screamed her brother's name and then looked up, fury written all over her pretty face.

"Why, you big gorilla! You'll be sorry you tangled with the Beaumonts!" Faster than I thought possible, she reached for one of the crates and hurled it at the man.

He dodged aside, his face registering shock. No sooner had the crate flown past than he had to duck to avoid an inkwell, a crowbar, and a steady stream of other detritus. Dora muttered furiously and grunted as she hurled everything she could reach at the man.

I took advantage of the distraction to pick up an empty porcelain vase and sneak up behind him. Then I waited for my chance and smashed it over his head. With great satisfaction, we watched as he crumpled to the ground.

"Did you kill him?" Dora gasped.

"I hope not."

"Well, I do. What are we going to do?"

I bit my lip. "We have to get out of here. Can you wake Charlie?"

Dora nodded and bent over her brother.

I'm not entirely sure why I did it, but I ran, not towards the door, but to the desk that had caught my eye earlier. I was certain that this was the desk used by the boss, which meant that the account book sitting on top of it was likely to hold information about the smuggling operation. If my hunch was right, it would be an incredibly valuable piece of evidence.

Charlie awoke with a groan and Dora helped him sit up.

"Can you walk?" she asked. "They'll be back any moment. We have to hide until Gus brings the police."

She helped her brother to his feet and he swayed unsteadily.

"Come on, Ruby," Dora called.

"You go ahead. I'll be right behind you."

"Hurry," she called unnecessarily and steered Charlie out the door.

I nodded and flipped open the account book. It was stupid of me to waste time. I should have picked up the book and hustled back towards the door, following Dora and Charlie to safety. But my mind was whirling and I paused to scan the book to see if it was worth stealing.

The writing was tidy and the accounting meticulous. I froze, my eyes wide. I'd seen this handwriting before. The writing in this book was exactly like the church ledger. I looked at the cat statue sitting on the edge of the desk and suddenly remembered the figurine that had been in Mrs. Mills' bag along with the ledger. It had also been a cat statue.

Noise in the hallway pulled me out of my shock before I

had time to discern whether there was some logical explanation for why Mrs. Mills had one of these cat statues in her bag and why she'd clearly been the one to fill out this account book. I looked around for a place to hide.

Spotting a door, I picked up the book and scampered across the room. The door led to a storage room of some kind and I ducked inside, closing the door just as the people from the hall entered the office.

"George!" a man's voice called. I figured he must have seen his compatriot lying unconscious on the floor.

"Where are they?" a woman's voice asked, so commandingly that I almost didn't recognize it.

"They must have escaped," Hardy replied. "They can't have gotten far. Don't worry, Mrs. Mills, we'll find them."

"You'd better find them, you fool. And when you do, get rid of them."

I put a hand over my mouth to cover my gasp of horror. I don't know if I was more afraid for my friends or more shocked that Ida Mills was the head of the drug ring. There was no point in trying to explain away the ledger or the statues. Here was undeniable evidence of her guilt.

"Do you want us to bring them to you like we did with Jean?" asked Hardy.

"No, just finish them off. I wanted Jean to see me and know that I was the one who was killing her. No one threatens me and gets away with it. That's why I had you bring her to that alley and why I used my own scarf to do the job. These three foolish children are nothing more than an irritation." Mrs. Mills walked to her desk and the chair creaked as she sat down. "What are you standing around for? Go get them!"

Ida Mills had killed Jean? I couldn't reconcile that with the funny, shrewd woman I'd met at church. I'd wanted to find Jean's killer, but I was crushed that it was someone I'd liked so well. Was I such a poor judge of character that I hadn't seen the truth about Ida?

The men ran off, the sound of their shoes on the stairs fading away. I whispered a prayer that Charlie and Dora had found a good hiding place. With any luck, the police would be here soon and we'd be saved.

"Where is it?" Ida muttered. Then she cursed and got to her feet. Her heels clicked as she moved around the room, opening drawers and moving things around.

I held my breath as the echo of her steps began to move in my direction. She was looking for the account book! I looked down at it in horror. Why hadn't I left it on her desk?

Her shoes sounded outside my door and I held my breath. The door flew open and I found myself staring, mouth open, at Mrs. Ida Mills.

"Ruby! What in the world?" She stared at me in shock. Then her eyes slid down to the account book in my hands and a calculating expression blossomed on her face. "What are you doing with my ledger?"

I briefly considered bluffing my way out of trouble, but I didn't think I was a good enough liar to pull that off.

"I know you're the head of the drug ring," I said with as much bravado as I could muster.

"I see." She stepped back and motioned for me to come with her.

I followed warily as she walked back to her desk and pulled out a cigarette, lit it, and then sat in her chair, smoking. Looking back, I should have made a run for it, but in the moment, my curiosity and betrayal were too big to be ignored.

"I know you killed Jean Waldeck. I know you're smuggling drugs in those ugly cat statues. I think you're doing something with the money at church, though I'm not sure what." I took slow steps around her desk, positioning myself so that I had a clear pathway to the door. As much as I wanted to escape, I needed answers, too. Besides, the police should be arriving soon. Please, let them arrive soon!

Ida picked a piece of tobacco off her tongue and gave me a long look. "You're too smart for your own good, you know that? I should have known that any niece of Muriel Barnes' would be difficult."

For the first time, I felt a surge of pride in my aunt. "I suppose it runs in the family."

"Yes, I suppose it does. And that means that you're unlikely to be willing to be bought off. Hmmm? I could write you a check for a very large sum of money if you'll only keep your mouth shut."

"Are you going to kill my friends?" I was stalling for time now.

Ida chuckled. "There's really no other way. I can't have three nosy kids knowing my business. But you, Ruby, you could be useful. I could use a smart young woman like you to help me with my business."

"I'm not interested."

She raised an eyebrow. "No, I didn't expect you would be." Then Ida pulled open a drawer and withdrew a large revolver which she lifted and trained on me.

My heart began to gallop again. I lifted my hands and took a small step backwards, then another. "What were you doing with the church's bank account? Why would you deposit money into their account?"

"I don't see how it matters now. But I'll tell you if you really want to know. It's called money laundering. It would be suspicious if anyone ever examined my personal or business accounts and saw exactly how much money this particular work brings in. I deposit money in the church's account and no one knows it's mine."

That made sense. "Since you handle the accounts, no one knows how much you actually have deposited."

She cackled. "Why do you think a woman in this business would spend so much time at church suppers and playing bridge? People trust me there and give me free access to the bank account. So long as I can stand to spend time listening to sermons, I have a full set of character references. It's a brilliant cover."

Footsteps outside the door drew Ida's attention. Hardy stepped into the room and Ida lowered her gun momentarily.

"They might have got away," Hardy began.

I didn't wait to hear what Ida's replay was. I bolted for the door, dropping the account book as I ran. I think I jumped over the goon who was still lying unconscious on the floor in my haste to get away from Ida and her gun.

"Get her!" Ida's voice chased me down the hallway and I heard Hardy pounding behind me.

I reached the steps and looked down into the face of the other thug. With Hardy coming right behind me, there was only one direction to go. I grabbed the railing and began to climb up to the loft above.

CHAPTER FOURTEEN

The loft was filled with odds and ends, but they didn't offer as many hiding places as one might have hoped. Drop cloths covered bulky items but had little extra room to hide a desperate woman. Stacks of old newspapers seemed more likely to topple over than to provide cover. The work table against the far wall was the best spot I could find and I dived under it just before Hardy crested the edge of the loft.

Now I knelt in its shadowy underbelly with my heart pounding so loudly that I was sure he would hear it. He carefully moved across the loft floor and I saw that he had his pistol out. One wrong move and I would be dead. I'd never been so afraid in my entire life.

"Come on out and we'll talk," Hardy called. "There's no way to escape. If you come out now, maybe you'll get lucky and I'll let you work out a deal."

There wasn't a chance that was going to happen. I crouched and tried to quiet my breathing. Movement out of the corner of my eye drew my gaze towards the wall. Through the shadows, I thought I saw someone hiding behind a piece of equipment covered in a white canvas, covering along the back of the loft.

I closed my eyes and groaned silently. Oh, no! Were the Beaumonts trapped up here too? I'd been hoping that they somehow had escaped, and now we were all good and truly caught. Our only hope was that Gus and the police would arrive soon. So much time had passed, though, that I wondered if they would ever arrive.

Suddenly, a towering pile of broken crates crashed down over Hardy. I watched as he ducked, throwing his arms over his head. Whether or not the fall had been intentional, Dora was revealed in the space where the crates had once been. She tried to dart away, but Hardy was too fast. His arm shot out and got hold of Dora, wrapping around her neck.

Hardy pulled her to his chest and pressed his gun to her temple. "Come out, you two, or she gets it."

Since he planned to kill Dora no matter what, it seemed like a silly threat. I bit my lip and considered my options. Would Hardy keep her alive longer if we stayed out of sight?

He must have realized that we weren't going to bite. He snarled, "Tell you what: if you come out now, I'll kill her fast. If you make me wait, I'll make sure her death is long and painful and that you have to watch before I do the same to you."

That threat frightened me into action since I had no doubt that he would do it. I climbed out from under the table and began to walk forward slowly, hands in the air. I tried to keep something between us at all times. If I thought he was going to shoot, I might have just enough time to duck behind the pile of broken crates or the bags of sawdust.

"You won't get away with this," I called. "Our friend

went to the police a half hour ago. They should be arriving any minute. If you leave now, you might be able to get away."

"Sure, sure." Hardy thought it was a bluff. "You must think I'm really stupid to give me a story like that."

I shook my head. "I think you're cruel and evil and shrewd, but I know you're not stupid."

My mind raced to find a new topic to keep him busy. The soft movement behind me announced that Charlie was on the move. I needed to get Hardy to turn towards where the loft ended, with his back to the piles of junk where Charlie was stalking. Trying not to be obvious, I drifted closer to where the loft dropped off. Luckily, Hardy followed, mirroring my actions.

"You know, Dora Beaumont's parents are very wealthy. If you let us go, they'll pay you a lot."

Hardy laughed and opened his mouth to give me some nasty retort, but Charlie leaped forward and grabbed him from behind by the throat. Sputtering with rage and shock, Hardy let go of Dora and dropped his gun, which skittered harmlessly out of his reach. Dora hadn't known her brother was about to pounce and was startled. She fell to her knees only a few inches from where the loft floor stopped and empty air began.

"Dora!" I screamed as I dove for her.

My friend teetered for a second that lasted for hours. She wasn't so close to the edge that she was in imminent danger, but she was caught off guard as well as being tipsy. I knew that it wouldn't take much for her to fall.

As I scrambled across the floor, I reached the gun and knocked it over the side of the loft. It wasn't the smartest move, since I didn't know where Ida or the other thug were, but I wasn't about to pick it up and use it, so I figured it would be better off out of Hardy's reach. I reached Dora only a moment later and hugged her tightly, pulling her away from the dangerous drop.

Charlie and Louis grappled close to us. Hardy had gotten loose and was trying to swipe at Charlie with a knife he'd pulled from some secret location. From our place on the ground, Dora and I watched the progress of the fight. Too worried about Charlie to consider leaving, we screamed warnings and advice as Hardy lunged and Charlie dodged. Several times, the two drew near to the edge of the loft and I was afraid they'd tumble over.

Suddenly, the warehouse doors slid open and several uniformed men strode in. My fear instantly turned into exhausted relief.

The appearance of the policemen interrupted the brawl. Charlie looked up and grinned. Hardy, knowing he was about to be caught, made a final desperate lunge at Charlie with the knife. Without realizing it, the pair had moved much closer to the edge, though it was Charlie whose back was to the two-story drop and whose heels were only inches from it.

Charlie was able to sidestep Hardy's lunge and the knife nicked his arm as the smuggler flew past. Instinctively, Charlie reached for the other man as he tipped over the edge. For one moment that seemed frozen in time, the pair balanced in the air. Hardy leaned back over the empty air and Charlie gripped his arm.

Then the momentum shifted and Charlie began to lean forward. Hardy's face filled with fear and he tried desperately to find a way to stop the inevitable. But there was nothing he could do. The arm in Charlie's grip slipped until his fingers held only air and Hardy fell with a horrible shriek to the concrete floor below, where he landed with a crunch that I knew would haunt me.

I almost didn't hear his landing because Charlie was now falling forward. He dropped to his knees and rolled, but his legs were off the edge of the loft floor before he was able to slow himself, his fingers holding desperately to a groove in the flooring.

Instantly, I jumped up and clambered over to him, Dora crawling beside me.

"Hold one, Charlie, the police are coming," I gasped. "Don't give up, they're almost here."

Charlie's wild, fearful eyes found mine and he nodded, resolve creasing his forehead. I lay as flat as I could and gripped his arm above the elbow. Dora mirrored me on the other side. He was sweating and his shirt was growing slick.

"He's slipping!" Dora cried.

"Don't let go!" I grunted, trying to get a better hold on him. "They're almost here!"

Policemen were shouting and rushing to get to us. I prayed that we could hold Charlie long enough. The police were so close!

Charlie let out a strangled cry and his fingers were suddenly scrambling, scratching to catch hold. I felt him slip out of my grasp and Dora screamed. Then she was clutching at empty air, his arm having slid out from between her hands.

"No!" The scream tore at my throat and I knew in that instant that I couldn't hold on any longer.

A figure dove past me and just managed to grab Charlie's hand as it slipped over the edge. I rolled to the side, out of the way of the police, and saw that Gus had arrived in time and caught Charlie. He grimaced as Charlie dangled from his hand, 20 feet above the cement floor below. Ted

Grey and another officer positioned themselves hastily and added their strength to help heave Charlie slowly over the edge.

I rolled onto my back in the dust and burst into tears. It was over. We'd survived.

Ted found a blanket for Dora and sat with her while she cried. His superior, Sergeant Sandercock, took me aside for questioning while a plainclothes detective got Charlie's side of the story. As the sergeant grilled me, I had to make sure to stand where I couldn't see the sheet covering Hardy's dead body. One glance in that direction and I started shaking again.

Ida Mills was in handcuffs, along with both of her thugs, one looking slightly cross- eyed from the blow I'd given him. The three were led to police cars and driven away. Ida made a point not to spare me even the smallest of glances.

"What were you kids doing here?" The sergeant lifted his eyebrows and gave me a fatherly scowl.

"I'll have to start at the beginning," I decided. "I under-stand that you've been investigating Jean Waldeck's murder. Is that right?"

His eyebrows shot up. "How do you know that?"

I took a deep breath and began the story. I explained about how we'd known that Jean wasn't just out for a walk and that she hadn't been robbed. Soon, he changed from disbelieving to convinced and took avid notes as I described our meeting with Liam and what we'd learned from Gord Waldeck. I reminded him of the attacks on Gus and me. Then I explained why we were at the warehouse and what we'd learned from Louis Hardy before his death.

In the recitation, I didn't mention that we'd been at a party with Jean the night of her death or that we'd suspected Mr. Beaumont of running the drug ring.

"Would you swear in court that Mrs. Mills confessed to killing Jean Waldeck?" the sergeant checked.

"I would." Despite the absolute terror I'd experienced that evening and the dead body lying only yards away, I felt proud of us. We'd known something was wrong and fought until we uncovered the truth.

I searched for Charlie and saw him leaning into the crate and pulling up a plaster cat to show the detective. Telling the police everything took much longer than I expected, but finally we were free to go home. Charlie offered Gus a ride to Aunt Muriel's for a hot drink. We were all dying to hear Gus's side of the story and knew he would want to hear everything from us.

"What in the world is going on?" Aunt Muriel demanded as we strode into the house.

I looked around at us and had to admit that we looked a sight. My poor aunt was probably going to have to scrub the house down after we left. I knew I was covered in dust and sweat after hiding in the loft. Charlie had a spreading bruise and a swelling knot on the side of his head. Dora's hair was all over the place and her stockings were torn. Even Gus looked the worse for wear with his shirttails hanging out and a button missing from his slide across the loft floor.

"We've had an adventure tonight you'll hardly believe," I began, and we all sank gladly onto the furniture.

Aunt Muriel's eyes grew wide and her mouth became the thinnest of lines as I told her everything. There were parts that no one else knew. I explained about how we knew that Jean had been intentionally murdered, how Gus had helped me figure out about the poisoning at church, and what I'd seen in the church ledger. I told everyone about the strange deposit and was glad when they looked as confused as I'd been. We told Aunt Muriel about the visit to Gord Waldeck, what we'd learned from Liam, and our suspicions about the warehouse.

When we got to the part about the warehouse, I sat back and eagerly listened to Charlie and Dora describe how they'd been chased upstairs and hidden while the men searched down below.

"They thought we had run outside," Charlie explained, "but we knew we wouldn't get far on foot."

Then it was my turn to tell them what had happened with Ida in the office.

Aunt Muriel sniffed once I finished that part and I could almost feel the waves of superiority coming off of her. "I could have told you that Ida was no good."

I blinked at her. "How did you know that?"

"She dyes her hair," Aunt Muriel said in such a matter-of-fact tone that we all stared at her for several seconds before I gathered myself enough to change the subject.

"Gus, what happened when you went for the police?"

He took a deep breath and began tiredly. "Things were pretty quiet when I got to the station. It took some convincing to get the gumshoe behind the desk to believe that I was serious."

"But you convinced him in the end, right?" I pressed.

"Sure. You know you can count on your old pal Gus. Of course, the trouble was that the fuzz was already out breaking up some speakeasy they'd found. We had to wait for everyone to come back before we could head back to the warehouse. I was in a lather by the time we left. I thought for sure you'd all have been taken for a ride and be sleeping with the fishes."

The look he gave me was very warm and I hoped that he meant that he was especially grateful that I was all right.

"It's a good thing you got there when you did," Charlie sighed. "I can't believe how close I came to dropping off the edge of the loft."

"What in the world?" Aunt Muriel asked sharply, her eyes pinning him. "How did that happen?"

Dora explained how we'd all ended up in the loft and how Hardy had appeared. She said that she hadn't intended to knock over the crates, but her foot had bumped them and over they went. I thought that she must still be rattled after the evening's events, since the Dora I knew wouldn't have admitted to making a mistake.

As Charlie described his fight with Hardy, my stomach knotted again as he told Aunt Muriel how he'd slowly lost his grip. I knew I'd have nightmares about him falling for a long time to come.

Once we'd relived the entire story, we sat back in silence.

"Ida Mills killed Jean Waldeck," Aunt Muriel said quietly, and shook her head.

"And she was behind the drug smuggling ring." I reached out and took my aunt's hand. Even though the two hadn't been close, Ida had betrayed everyone at Aunt Muriel's church. She'd been here in this house and she was a criminal. It was a strange feeling.

Aunt Muriel squeezed my hand and looked over at me. "They wouldn't have caught her so soon without your help, Ruby. I'm proud of you."

I gave her a tired smile. "Thank you, Aunt Muriel. That means a lot to me. I'm glad you were willing to let me come and live here with you. I've had more adventure here in Port Vernon than I ever imagined.

"And it's just the beginning!" Dora piped up. "I know we'll solve many more mysteries together."

Charlie and Gus hooted with laughter.

"How do you know that?" Charlie poked her in the ribs. "Are you announcing that you're now clairvoyant?"

Dora beamed around at the room. "No, but our summer house is haunted! We'll have to go there this summer and see if Ruby can figure out why the ghost won't leave us alone."

We all burst into laughter. I doubted that Dora was serious, though, knowing her, it was a definite possibility. Still, the possibility of further mysteries filled me with anticipation. Maybe I wouldn't investigate ghosts, but I did hope that there would be more puzzles that needed figuring out and more people I could help.

Dora said, "Well, Ruby? What do you think?"

I grinned at her. "I guess we'll see what happens next."

PLEASE LEAVE A REVIEW

Enjoy this book? As an indie publisher, reviews are so important to us.

You can help by letting us know what you think.

Please leave a review on Amazon by visiting your recent orders page or searching for the title of this book.

Thank you!

—Kyla at Cinnamon Cozies

ABOUT THE AUTHOR

Beth Brinkmeyer is a librarian at an elementary school in South Carolina. She's been a lover of mysteries since she first read "The Boxcar Children." Her favorite mysteries include Nancy Drew, Trixie Belden, Agatha Christie (of course), and Anne Perry. In addition to reading both for fun and for work, Beth crochets, is very involved with her church, and hangs out with her hunky husband, Ben. Like Ruby Martin, Beth's own father was a pastor as well as a missionary which mean that her family has lived in Taiwan, Canada, and all around the U.S. Beth and her husband are in the process of adopting a child from India.